THE HOUSE OF DEATH

THE HOUSE OF DEATH

Book 2 of *The Harem Conspiracy*

BRUCE BALFOUR

Scribbling Gargoyle

Books by Bruce Balfour

<u>HISTORICAL NOVELS</u>
The River of Eternity (Book 1 of The Harem Conspiracy)
The House of Death (Book 2 of The Harem Conspiracy)
The Revenge of Sekhmet (Book 3 of The Harem Conspiracy) –
coming soon

<u>SCIENCE FICTION NOVELS</u>
The Forge of Mars
The Digital Dead (sequel to *The Forge of Mars*)
Prometheus Road (Young Adult)

<u>THRILLER NOVELS</u>
Burning Season

Author's Note

I have attempted to be as accurate as possible regarding locations, historical figures, religious proceedings, judicial processes, and other minutiae of New Kingdom Egypt, and I apologize in advance for any factual errors in rendering the reality of the ancient world. Many of the characters are drawn from the oldest written record of a judicial proceeding that we have, commonly known as the Harem Conspiracy, relating to the attempted assassination of Pharaoh Ramesses III. This story begins well before the Harem Conspiracy, and some characters are fictional, but I hope I have accurately portrayed what it was like to live during that period.

As in modern society, the ancient Egyptians didn't approve of some kinds of daily violence, while other kinds were considered appropriate and necessary. As an example, we have court proceedings, letters, and other official texts from later periods of Egyptian history that document sanctioned corporal punishments: beatings for failure to pay taxes, beatings for students who failed to study, inflicting open wounds for theft or failure to pay debts, mutilation, and execution. A criminal found to have stolen food from temple lands, tomb robbing, or having minor involvement in the Harem Conspiracy might have their nose and ears removed. A more extreme crime could lead to impalement "on the wood," as depicted in this hieroglyphic determinative (from Daniel McClellan, Brigham Young University Ancient Near Eastern Studies Program) that explains itself pretty well:

Thanks for reading.

Bruce Balfour, PhD
Phoenix, Arizona
January, 2024

Do not lead a man astray with reed pen or papyrus document,
It is the abomination of God.
Do not witness a false statement,
Nor remove a man from the list by your order;
Do not enroll someone who has nothing,
Nor make your pen be false.
If you find a large debt against a poor man,
Make it into three parts;
Release two of them and let one remain:
You will find it a path of life;
You will pass the night in sound sleep; in the morning
You will find it like good news.
Better it is to be praised as one loved by men
Than wealth in the storehouse;
Better is bread when the mind is at ease
Than riches with troubles.

--From the wisdom text, *Instruction of Amenemope*
(Hieratic copy ca. 1300-1075 BCE, New Kingdom Egypt: by
Amenemope son of Kanakht.
Translated from British Museum Papyrus 10474 by E.A. Wallis
Budge in 1924.)

One

1184 BCE—Thebes

Year 4 of His Majesty, King of Upper and Lower Egypt, Chosen by Re, Beloved of Amun, Pharaoh Setnakhte, Second Month of Akhet (Season of Inundation), Day 18

#

Khenti and Ruta followed the same route from the Valley of the Kings to the river that they had used successfully on their first trip. The sled was heavier this time since Khenti had widened the tunnel opening enough to get larger gold and silver objects out of the tomb. Only one Medjay patrol passed them in the darkness, and then they were past the high point of their trail and it was easier dragging the sled down the long slope to the tall reeds of the river bank. With his usual timing, Neferabu met them at just the right moment to avoid having to drag the heavy sled any farther. He had, however, arranged for the Greek trading boat to meet them at the pyramid rocks once more.

"It will be our old friend, Thales, again," Neferabu said, making a little bed out of the reeds so that he could rest. "He has three boats with him on this trip, with just enough room left to take tonight's cargo. The rest of what we dig up will have to be sold to someone else. Or we can wait a few months until Thales returns from the Great Green."

While Neferabu settled himself down and closed his eyes, Khenti looked up into the partial face of the moon-god, Khonsu. "Perhaps we should stop."

Neferabu sat up, his eyes alert. "Stop? Why?"

"Because this is a dangerous occupation," Khenti said. "Because it's hard work digging at night after I spend the day digging somewhere else. Because I'm tired!"

"Quiet," Neferabu whispered. "Keep your voice down."

"Will you listen to me if I do?"

"Of course, my old friend. I always listen to you. And I understand how tired you must be. What if I help you dig?"

"Not to offend, Nef, but you're an artist, not a quarryman. Your arms are small and weak. You would only be in my way in the small spaces of the tomb."

"Ruta helps you," Neferabu said, pointing at the silent boy watching them with wide eyes.

"Yes. He drags rocks out of the tunnel. He scampers like a ferret among the rubble and carries small things to the sled. He brings me water. So, you see, I don't need your help in the tomb."

"Ah, but can he help you lift the heavy things? Can he entertain you with his amusing stories? These are things only I can do."

Ruta stuck his tongue out at Neferabu, but then he smiled. His teeth glowed in the moonlight.

Khenti sighed. "I don't know. It seems to me that the longer we spend digging in the tomb, the more likely it is that the

Medjay will find us. Or the necropolis priests. I'm a simple man—I don't wish to be impaled on a stick or have my nose and ears removed. I like them right where they are."

"Just think of the wealth we'd be leaving behind, Khenti. Think of all we could do with it. We could live like pharaohs our-selves with nice houses, our own harems, many children, plenty of food, and our own harems."

"You said harems twice."

Neferabu smiled. "Maybe I did. A man can always use more than one harem. And what about your family? I know you're thinking of your widowed mother and what she'll need now that her husband is gone. And your sisters can't support themselves. They all depend on you. What would it hurt to give them a little more than you had planned?"

Khenti slapped at a big mosquito on his arm. "I must think on this."

"That's all I ask. I'm sure that my old friend will arrive at the best decision for himself, for me, and for his family. Not to forget little Ruta here." Neferabu said, patting the boy's head.

The sound of wood scraping along the reeds warned them that the boat was coming. A silhouette appeared against the moon. The boat was about the same size as the last one with two masts and the same gaudy decorations painted on the outside. Neferabu stood so that he could help tie the mooring line to the pyramid rocks.

While a sailor helped Neferabu into the boat, Khenti and Ruta started removing things from the sled to speed the unload-ing. They had been fortunate so far to avoid the Medjay patrols, but he didn't want to push their luck. A few minutes later,

Neferabu and the sailors brought nets to help them load the cargo onto the boat. Thales watched the entire process from the bow with a big smile on his face.

Ruta was just going back for two gold *ushabti* figures—servants intended to help the tomb owners in the afterlife—when he heard the sound of a chariot moving slowly toward them on the the path beside the river. Leaving the gold figures behind on the sled, he turned and ran back to the boat to tell Khenti and Neferabu what he had heard.

Thales reacted quickly. A sword appeared in his hand, which alarmed Khenti and Neferabu, but he used it to cut the mooring line that secured the boat to the pyramid rocks. Motioning for his passengers to remain quiet, he disappeared beyond the cargo stacked on the deck. The boat turned in graceful silence and moved off toward the middle of the river.

When they were a safe distance away from the bank, Thales returned with what appeared to be two big jugs of beer cradled in his arms. "Your payment, my friends. It has been a profitable evening for all of us."

Khenti wondered why they were being paid in beer, but he started to catch on when he noticed the loud thump each jug made when Thales set them down on a crate in front of them. Neferabu smiled and reached inside one of them, withdrawing a handful of silver ingots and gold rings. As each one dropped back into the jug, it made a metallic *tink*! sound.

"Music to my ears," Neferabu said.

Khenti looked into the other jug and saw shiny things in the moonlight. He plucked out one of the rings and put it on Ruta's thumb, which made him smile. "Shiny!"

"I don't think the patrol saw us, so I'll drop you off at a safe distance downriver," Thales said. The jugs are heavy, but it shouldn't be too far for you to hike back to your village."

Remembering his appointment, Khenti looked up. "Perhaps you could let me off at the main landing in Thebes? I'd like to spend some of my earnings tonight."

"Of course, of course," Thales said with a broad smile. "A man needs his little celebrations of life, eh?"

Neferabu didn't look convinced. "Are you sure that's wise, Khenti? Someone will see you if you wait until morning to go back to the village from Thebes. We don't want to draw any suspicion."

"I understand. I'll be back before the *Manzet-boat* of the dawn rises above the horizon."

"Then maybe I should go with you. Thebes can be a rough place at night."

Khenti smiled and shook his head. "Thank you for your offer, Nef. I'd actually prefer some privacy where I'm going."

Thales laughed, nudged Neferabu in the side, and winked at Khenti. "Try not to spend it all in one place, my friend."

#

After all the years he'd spent carrying stone out of the tombs, like his ancestors before him, Khenti looked powerful enough that few people would bother him in the streets of Thebes at night. Despite that, the big clay jar that he carried would have been certain to draw the attention of risk-takers who would try to take it away from him if anyone could have seen the silver and gold that it contained.

The buildings still burned with the heat that they had

absorbed during the day, but he felt a pleasant current of cooler air blowing past his bare legs while he strolled toward the administrative core of the city. Enough torches, temple braziers, and oil lamps continued to burn to light his way along the stinking streets. He knew he was drawing close to the residence he sought when he passed the House of Kifi, where two young women smiled at him from the front doorway and beckoned him inside. Continuing on, he passed the home of the vizier and arrived at the door belonging to the three-story house of Mayor Paweraa.

Diligent knocking eventually roused one of the slaves, who opened the door just enough to peer outside. Khenti saw only one eye and part of a man's face.

"Who dares to disturb the residence of his lordship, Mayor Paweraa?" asked a grumpy male voice.

"Tell him Khenti is here."

The slaved looked doubtful.

"Khenti, Quarryman of Pharaoh on the Right Side in the Great Place of the western horizon. I have a delivery that he requested."

"A delivery? Then leave it by the door and I'll bring it in after you're gone."

"I must place this delivery in his hands myself," Khenti said, holding up the heavy jar. "And your punishment will be great if you don't tell your lord that I'm here waiting for him."

The slave took a step back, studied him for a moment, then shrugged. "All right. I'll get him. But don't say I didn't warn you."

Before he scuttled away, the slave allowed him through the door into a pleasant courtyard with two trees overshadowing a small pond. The face of the moon-god was reflected in the still water. On the other side of the pond, Paweraa's stately home loomed over his head. A few minutes later, the mayor himself shuffled out into the yard, yawning and blinking. Whenever he saw the mayor, Khenti thought how large his head looked compared to his body, even though he had the round shape of a well-fed city administrator who rarely, if ever, had to labor outside.

"Khenti, my good friend, it's always a pleasure to see you, but my heart would be filled with much more joy if you had delighted me with your presence in the morning."

Khenti nodded his head and held out the clay jar. "Unfortunately, my movements are restricted during the day. I have a delivery for you, my lord."

Paweraa's eyes widened and he beckoned Khenti into the house. They entered his spacious audience room, cooled by high windows just below the ceiling, and Khenti studied the fancy chair of ebony wood centered on the raised dais. The chair was inset with colored stones to form a scene of a man hunting from his boat with a long spear among the river weeds. Paweraa dismissed the slave that Khenti had met at the front door, then settled into the big chair with a grunt. However, he jumped up again when Khenti emptied the contents of the jar on the dais. Gold and silver clattered onto the wood platform.

"May you live a long life of good health and prosperity, Khenti! Is this my share of the proceeds from our little enterprise?"

"Half of it is yours, my lord."

"You have done well! Very well, indeed!" Paweraa's eyes glittered and danced as he stared at the pile with a big smile. "The great Amun-Re, king of the gods, has smiled upon us this day.

And how fortunate you must think you were to have met me, eh? Without my map and my knowledge of the best tombs, you'd be forced to spend your life breaking rocks deep beneath the earth!"

Khenti nodded. "I humbly appreciate your wisdom and trust in me, my lord. I know that the great Amun-Re must love me, for he has allowed us to meet and become wealthier for having met."

Paweraa's fingers twitched until he finally kneeled beside their pile of earnings and ran his hand through the shiny rings and bars. Khenti felt fortunate that Thales had been able to pay with valuable metals since it would have been time-consuming and awkward to lead cattle or goats or carry bags of grain or other goods of equal value. He couldn't *eat* the metals, of course, but grain was easy to come by when one could afford it.

"Yes, we are favored by the gods," Paweraa said, looking up at Khenti with a serious expression. "And it would be unfortunate to lose the great wealth that we've acquired, would it not?"

"Of course, my lord," Khenti said with a frown. "Why do you say this?"

The metals clinked together as Paweraa stirred his fingers through them. "Although I don't know why, Vizier To has become suspicious that tomb robberies are increasing in the Great Place. You know as well as I that the treasures of the long-dead nobles are no longer of use to them. Wealth is wasted if it's buried permanently under the ground. With each piece that we bring to the light, the more prosperity is returned to the people of Thebes. However, not everyone is so enlightened and progressive in their views. Men are still impaled upon the wood when the magistrates find them guilty of tomb robbing."

Khenti didn't like this kind of talk. "Then I should stop and seal up the tomb again."

Paweraa waved his hands. "No, no, no! Let's not be hasty. There will be time enough for that later. In the meantime, we must redouble our efforts to ensure that our futures will be secure, prosperous, healthy, and safe. Our wives, our children, our parents—they all depend on us to give them good lives. And we deserve to live well ourselves! While the gods continue to smile on us, we must work even harder to bring more treasures to light."

"But, my lord, you say that Vizier To is aware of us!"

"I said no such thing, young Khenti. I said he is merely suspicious of the activity in the Great Place. I thought you might hear of this from other sources and I didn't want you to panic. Tomb objects have been appearing for sale in the local markets, and they could only have come from one place."

Khenti gasped. "I was told that they'd only be sold in Greece!"

Paweraa shrugged. "Such is the way of traders and merchants, Khenti. They cannot be trusted. They seek profits as quickly as they possess a thing. But we must not let this deter us from our efforts, for I have a solution that will focus Vizier To's eyes on other likely offenders."

"How is that possible? Are there others working for you? Or are there others digging among the ancient tombs? I've seen no sign of such activity."

"Leave these things to me, Khenti," he said, resting a fatherly hand on Khenti's shoulder. "There is an answer for every problem."

#

Mayor Paweraa always enjoyed making the Medjay police kneel when they entered the audience hall of his elegant home. Sermont, in particular, needed to be reminded of his lower status, otherwise he would become uncontrollable. The stonecutter, Khenti, had made his delivery an hour before Sermont's arrival, giving Paweraa time to summon the police captain and develop a plan to intercept some of the problems that were developing in his life. His ability to plan for potential unfortunate events had always been the key to success in his career, and he had no desire to have his nose and ears cut off, or to die upon the stake, for his small part in redistributing the wealth from a forgotten tomb. However, the purchasers of the stolen goods had shown poor judgment by selling their wares in Thebes, bringing the tomb robbery to the awareness of Paweraa's superior, Vizier To. The vizier, an ambitious man who took his job seriously, always sought swift justice for those who would defile the tombs of the Great Place. The Medjay were already under orders to increase their patrols of the west bank tombs and to conduct investigations into any rumors of unusual activity among the tomb workers. Therefore, a tomb defiler had to be found. Khenti was too valuable a worker to sacrifice, and he might reveal Paweraa's part in the robbery if he were tortured during his interrogation.

"May the light of Re shine upon you, my lord mayor," Sermont said, kneeling in front of Paweraa's chair on its raised dais. "How can I be of assistance at this dark and very late hour of the night?"

"You have many talents, Sermont. You never sleep, you have no hesitation when it comes to violence, your mind is clean and uncluttered by complex thoughts, and you have flexible morals."

Uncomfortable kneeling on the hard floor tiles, Sermont nodded and started to rise, but Paweraa motioned for him to stay down.

"These are all excellent qualities, Sermont. A man in your line of work could have a very successful career by applying his talents for me when special situations arise."

Sermont smiled. "I am ever at your service, my lord mayor."

"Of course you are. You're like one of Pharaoh's faithful greyhounds, ever ready to kill something and bring it back to Pharaoh for his next meal. And you should be rewarded for such faithful devotion to your craft. You may stand up."

Sermont nodded and stood up.

Paweraa gestured at a dark wood chest inlaid with ivory at the edge of the dais. "Open the chest and remove what you find inside."

When Sermont lifted the lid, his eyes widened. He removed three objects fashioned in the old style: a female ushabti figure made of ebony wood and electrum, a pair of formal sandals inlaid with gold and precious stones, and a hawk pectoral on a gold chain with blue and green stones set in its spread wings. When he was able to tear his eyes away from the objects, which were probably the most valuable items he'd ever touched, the look of hope in his eyes was almost enough to tug at Paweraa's heart.

"For me?" Sermont whispered.

"Don't be a fool, Sermont. I could buy the services of a Medjay army with those. There are other rewards waiting for you once you've completed a task for me."

"What's that?"

"You must arrest Hapu the scribe."

Sermont frowned and tipped his head to the side, once again reminding Paweraa of a dog. "Happily. But why?"

Paweraa sighed and shook his head. "Some unfortunate news has come to my attention. Hapu is a greedy man. He lives in a big house with many servants and a family to support, and he somehow manages to do that on a scribe's earnings. You may wonder how this is possible?"

Sermont shrugged. "Scribes are paid well."

"Obviously, you've never been to Hapu's house. He lives well beyond his means. And now I know why." He pointed at the expensive tomb objects. "He robs the honored dead. He steals from the tombs of the nobles on the west bank."

Sermont gasped and took a step back. "Hapu? The scribe? He never does anything wrong."

"So you would think, but he's a very clever man, this Hapu. You saw how he humiliated you by making you release his son after you arrested him. How do you think he managed to do that?"

Sermont frowned. "You were the one who told me to release Ray."

"At Hapu's insistence," Paweraa said. "He has powerful friends, which is why you'll have to arrest him quietly. No one must know. His neighbors must not see you take him, and he must not have any visitors."

"Ah," said Sermont, pretending to understand.

Paweraa sighed. This was almost too easy.

"And what about Ray? Arrest him, too?"

"Ray is another matter. Do you recall hearing that the great General Hori, the most favored of Pharaoh's generals, sent a message to all the cities upriver from Pi-Ramesses?"

Paweraa watched in silence as Sermont shook his head. He obviously couldn't read, and he wasn't smart enough to pay attention to what was going on around him. Hori's message had been relayed along the command chain to the city administrators and the police units all along the Nile. However, since Sermont hadn't heard the news, he saw no need to go into details. Sermont could remain in the dark.

"Hori's message can be ignored for now. Hapu is your first priority. Leave the son free. Once you have Hapu in your custody, Ray will come to us, most likely with a hefty bribe to have his father released. We will confiscate the bribe as evidence against Hapu, then report to Vizier To that you've captured a tomb robber and a fugitive who flees from the wrath of the living god. I can assure you that the vizier, and General Hori, will be pleased."

#

Disdaining the big chair that dominated the reception hall of his house, Hapu sat on a leather stool at a small dining table beside his visitor, Khamenwati, the overseer and head teacher of the scribe school in Thebes. The ancient scribe leaned on his carved ivory ibis cane, a present that Pharaoh Setnakhte had given him in honor of the great god Thoth, the creator of language and writing. Khamenwati had been Setnakhte's teacher for many years, and Pharaoh still held a special place in his heart for the old curmudgeon, writing to him at least once a year to see how he and the school were doing in Thebes. Although he wasn't sure, Hapu felt that Khamenwati had also played a part in his receiving the summons from Pharaoh Ramesses III to be the special tutor for the royal children.

Three servants watched them from the serving tables loaded with roast meats, breads, and an array of fruits in bowls by the rear wall. Hapu held up his empty wine cup, prompting one of the servants to rush forward and refill it from a clay jug of wine. This being one of the nicer houses in Thebes, the wine jug itself was filled from the wine basin on the wall that always seemed magically full because of its connection to the larger reservoir in the kitchen. Hapu was proud of this "magical" feature, and his guests were often fascinated by it.

On the table before them, the evening meal remnants sat on their platters. A water jug and wash basin rested near their hands. Two oil lamps on the table enhanced the light from the four incense-burning braziers spaced evenly around the middle of the room near the blue wood pillars that held up the high ceiling. A cooling northerly breeze drifted through the high windows, swirling the clouds of incense and rippling the colorful woven tapestries that hung across three of the whitewashed walls.

"Have you had enough to eat?" Hapu asked, gesturing at the empty platters in front of Khamenwati while marveling at how much the thin old man could eat.

"If I needed more, I would ask for it," snapped the old teacher.

"Of course. More wine?"

Khamenwati held up his cup. It was quickly filled with wine

before the servant scuttled back to the rear of the hall. "And what news do you have of Pi-Ramesses, Hapu? How is Queen Isis?"

"Queen Isis is well, I believe. The living god Ramesses III has been away for some time defending our borders against the Tjehenu, so she's sad when he's away. Queen Teya is more independent and busy with her own projects, but she is also well. And as far as Setnakhte goes, you seem to know more about his ill health than I do."

Khamenwati frowned at Hapu, adding more wrinkles to his heavily lined face. "You say Queen Isis is well, *you believe*. What am I to make of that? Can't you answer a simple question?"

"She was well when last I saw her face. I cannot say how she is now."

"You dodge direct questions like a student who hasn't studied. When did you see her last?"

"About three weeks ago."

"Hmm. Are you being punished?"

Hapu blinked. "Why do you say that?"

"You're not in Pi-Ramesses. You didn't travel to the Beautiful Feast of Opet with the living god Setnakhte. Your son is here with you along with his strange friend. Since you're the royal tutor, who would normally be with the royal children every day, I have to suspect that you've done something wrong. Why are you here?"

Once again, Hapu was impressed with Khamenwati's perceptive nature. Although he disdained the trappings of royal power, he was always available when Vizier To, or Mayor Paweraa, or any of the nobles in Thebes needed advice about legal disputes or criminal activities that defied obvious solutions. Hapu had known that inviting Khamenwati to dinner at his home might be useful because he needed someone who could help him with the two boys in his care, but he also knew that Khamenwati might see through him before he could explain his real purpose for the dinner. The danger was that Khamenwati might misinterpret his actions and report Hapu to the Medjay, or even Vizier To. So, Hapu had chosen a cautious approach, reacquainting himself with the old teacher before telling him his secrets. Still, if something happened to Hapu, the boys would need someone they could depend on to help them, and he worried that Pasai would never come. If Khamenwati were on their side, he could hide and protect them until it was safe for them to return to Pi-Ramesses.

"Your tongue seems confused," Khamenwati said, leaning closer to stare into Hapu's eyes. "Are you here because of incompetence? Are your charges learning anything from you, or am I to find the Medjay at my door one day to punish me for my bad judgment in recommending you to Pharaoh?"

"The royal children are all brilliant and talented; voracious readers ready to learn."

Khamenwati snorted. "You're not justifying yourself to their father. Tell me the truth. I've never met a student who learned his lessons without motivation. As we have always known, a student scribe's ears are in his back, so he must be forced to listen by regular beatings with the cane."

"So it is said, but these are unusual children."

"You are merely getting soft in your old age," Khamenwati said. "You do them no favors by not beating them."

"Well, one must remember that they are the royal heirs of

Pharaoh. They are above the rules that govern the common people, and they inherit Pharaoh's divine abilities of thought and memory."

Khamenwati shook his head. "This explains why your own son has no manners. I can't blame him for not learning what he wasn't taught. I can only blame his teacher."

Hapu felt his face getting hot, but he needed the old teacher's help, so he kept his mind on the business at hand. "I need your assistance, teacher."

"Gotten yourself into trouble, have you?" Satisfied that he was getting to the root of the problem, Khamenwati pushed himself back with his cane and rested against the wall. "By the great beak of Thoth, what is it?"

"I know you hear things from your noble friends and parents of your students. Rumors of what goes on at court and among the nobles. Have you heard of anything unusual happening at Pi-Ramesses in recent weeks?"

"The living god's illness is the only thing I've noticed, but no one told me about it. I could see it for myself at the festival a few days ago. He didn't walk in the procession. Vizier To or the high priest might stand in for Pharaoh when he can't be present on normal occasions, but the Opet Festival is when Pharaoh's divine powers are renewed. The co-regent wasn't here, so I assumed he was away with the army, which is beyond Setnakhte's capacity these days. And that's all I know. The vizier has said that supply in the royal granaries is getting low, and Pharaoh is ready to raise taxes, but we have a good flood level this year, so all will be well in a few months. However, none of these things would seem to concern you. What have you done? Or is it your son who has offended Pharaoh?"

Hapu shook his head, wondering how much he should say. If no news of the attack on the palace had reached Thebes after all this time, then something odd was going on. It also raised the question of whether they should return to Pi-Ramesses to learn more. "I've done nothing wrong, teacher. Neither has my son. But the hostile forces of Set are abroad in this land of Kemet, and the world is out of balance—unless Pharaoh Setnakhte has brought Maat back to us."

"Hostile forces? I've heard nothing of these armies."

"No, because these are cowards who attack in the night. While the good god, Ramesses III, uses his mighty arm to defend our borders, others travel through our land protected by darkness. This is why I'm in Thebes with my son—and his friend." Hapu hesitated before saying any more.

Khamenwati's eyebrows arched over his dark eyes. "Pharaoh knows of this?"

"He must. His own golden house was attacked, although no one I've come across outside the palace seems to know of it. And I must be cautious with the people I ask about the event."

"And the princes? Where are they?"

Hapu knew it wouldn't take long for Khamenwati to start putting it all together. He would be a useful ally. However, before he could respond, they heard a distant argument in the courtyard. Alarmed, Hapu got up from the table. "Excuse me, Khamenwati."

Lost in his thoughts, Khamenwati shrugged and drank his wine while Hapu made his way out into the courtyard. On the other side of the rectangular pond, which was shaded by acacia, fig, pomegranate, and palm trees during the day, a high wall faced the street. One of his servants, Biti, stood behind the red granite door of the courtyard while peering through at the visitors beyond.

"I told you he can't be disturbed! He has a visitor dining with him this evening!"

As Hapu circled the pond, he saw Biti knocked backwards into the water as the granite door was forced open. Four Medjay policemen entered the courtyard, swords in hand, followed by their leader, Sermont.

"What do you think you're doing?" Hapu demanded, wishing he had some kind of a weapon.

Sermont smiled. "Hapu? How nice to see you again. Where is Ray?"

Hapu narrowed his eyes while the policemen started looking around in the courtyard. "He's not here. Why? Have you come to apologize?"

"Not here? How convenient. I've actually come to see you." Sermont studied the outside of the big house, the nice courtyard with its fruit trees, and the brass snakes that framed the door-ways. "Nice house for a scribe—even a famous one such as you. From what I've heard, you live as well as Pharaoh."

"Far from it. What do you want?"

"How does a scribe such as you earn enough to pay for a big house and all of its furnishings? And how do you pay the servants?"

"I work hard, Sermont, as I have for many years. You should try it sometime."

"Found one!" A burly policeman, with unusually good teeth, came rushing up to Sermont and offered him a gold *ushabti* figure that had probably been made for the tomb of a nobleman. "It was hidden in a corner of the yard behind a fig tree."

Before Hapu could say anything, another policeman ran up and handed Sermont a pair of sandals studded with precious stones. "My lord Sermont, these were found behind a water jar."

"Amazing what your men are able to find around my house," Hapu said, crossing his arms. "And so quickly. Are they doing so for a reason, or is this some sort of party game?"

"Oh, I assure you, Hapu, that this is no game. Serious charges have been made against you."

Hapu narrowed his eyes. "And what are these charges? Who made them?"

Sermont gestured and two of the policemen grabbed Hapu's arms. "This is a matter for the magistrate. I'm only here to collect you. I'm sure that my men would find more valuable objects hidden around your home, but we'll leave that for later. You're coming with us."

"Ridiculous! I'll go nowhere with you!" Hapu tried to retrieve his arms, but the policemen would not release him. He looked to Biti for assistance, but the servant was just rising from the pond when one of the other Medjay hit him over the back of the head and he collapsed on the sand. "Release me!"

Sermont patted Hapu's face with his palm. "I know you're an important man, Hapu, and I know you have important friends. But this time you've done something so bad that your friends can't help you. The magistrate will decide your fate. If you come with us quietly, I won't go into your house and look for your son right now. If not, I won't be able to restrain the enthusiasm of my men, who would certainly enjoy another visit with Ray. It's up to you."

"What guarantee do I have that you won't come back for my son later?"

Sermont sighed. "You misunderstand me, Hapu. There are no guarantees. If your son does something wrong, justice will find him, as I have found you. However, if you cooperate with us, his life may be easier—and probably longer than it will be if you don't."

Feeling trapped, but knowing that he could reason with the magistrate and get help from the mayor or the vizier once they learned of his situation, Hapu gritted his teeth and nodded.

#

Ray and Bull were outside the House of Kifi, where a naked woman danced in the doorway and beckoned them inside. A large Nubian played the drums behind her while keeping his back to the wall and his eyes on the two visitors. Ray's body longed for his bed and he swayed on his feet as if he were drunk. Their search for Tentopet had taken most of the night—starting at the Street of the Performers and continuing on through dozens of beer halls—but that was when many of their potential sources of information were awake. Previous searches during the day, when he was able to sneak out of his father's house, had uncovered nothing of her whereabouts. Finally, he had asked Bull to accompany him on a search at night, knowing that the streets were too dangerous for him to keep wandering around by himself, especially when he was still recovering from his last beating at the hands of the police. If Hapu discovered that he and Bull had sneaked out of the house at night, he knew he'd be punished severely, but his plan was to return early before Hapu had risen to bake the morning bread.

Once they entered the House of Kifi, smiling women appeared from every direction, many of them focused on Bull, who was physically more impressive than Ray. A girl who introduced herself as Harere took Ray by the hand and led them into a room where so much food and drink was heaped on the tables that Ray thought he was back in Pharaoh's palace.

"Please, eat as you wish," Harere said, gesturing at the table, and then sweeping her arm toward the many lovely women around the room who were smiling at them. "And consider your many choices this evening. Rest and take your time. Our mistress is occupied at the moment, but she will be in shortly to help you."

Harere released his hand as other women offered them two cups of wine with blue lotus flowers floating atop the liquid.

"Wait," Ray said, touching Harere's arm as she began to turn away. "I'm looking for someone in particular. Maybe you've seen her."

Ray described Tentopet. When he said Tentopet's name, the girl didn't seem to recognize it. Then he remembered to describe her and the last items of clothing he had seen her wearing. After a moment, Harere's eyes widened. "Tyti? You're looking for Tyti?"

Ray noticed that several of the women had backed Bull into a corner. Since he hadn't shown an interest in the lotus wine, they gave him a piece of turkey breast that he now consumed with great relish. Ray thought maybe he should interrupt, but he had other concerns at the moment. "Yes. Do you know Tyti?"

Harere looked around as if she didn't want to be heard, then she pulled Ray's face close to hers. "She was here. A Greek trader bought her. Thales."

Ray's heart leaped, but he tried to keep his voice low. "Yes! And she got away. Do you know where she might have gone to hide?"

Ray felt a light touch on his neck as a warm, liquid voice spoke to him from behind. "Young Harere is not available, my lord, but there are many others here who would enjoy spending time with you."

He stood up straight and turned around. The woman who stood in front of him looked as if she were a member of Pharaoh's harem with her exotic appearance and fine clothes. She held herself with the dignity of a queen as she studied his face with a slight, mysterious smile, and he felt that a man might easily fall into her deep brown eyes.

"I'm seeking one woman in particular—" Ray began before Harere poked him in the back.

"We have many to choose from," Apollonia said. "Perhaps your favorite is among them?"

"Well, no, apparently not," he said, hesitating when Harere tapped him on the back.

Apollonia frowned in a lovely way. "A few of the women are busy. Perhaps if you wait a while, you'll see the one you want. In the meantime, I think your companion has found several new friends. If he has the price, they can all spend time with him."

"I don't think so," Ray said, noting that he could barely see the top of Bull's head among the mass of women who surrounded him now. He'd have to rescue him soon.

"You don't think you have the price, or you don't think you wish to wait?"

Ray shrugged. "We have no money."

Any sign of Apollonia's smile vanished immediately. She raised her hand and two Nubian men appeared from out of nowhere. Moments later, he found himself on his face in the sandy street. Groaning, he rolled on his side and found Bull sitting beside him with a confused expression. "You okay, Bull?"

"Not friends," Bull said, pointing at the doorway blocked by the two Nubians.

"No. Not friends," Ray said.

Dejected, Ray led Bull back to Hapu's house. He hoped it was still early enough that Hapu had not risen to bake the morning bread. Just in case, they would enter at the side of the courtyard where the branch of a large tree hung over the wall. Ray had used the same tree as a child. However, as they passed the courtyard entrance, Ray saw that the red granite door was partially open. Biti was always careful about locking the door at night, so the fact that it was open made Ray suspicious. He looked around the street. Without any moonlight, he saw only shadows within shadows, but he felt as if they were being watched.

He put his hand on Bull's arm to get his attention and motioned for him to follow.

"Stay quiet," Ray whispered.

Bull followed Ray through the red granite door, which scraped on its hinges when he pushed it open. The courtyard itself looked as it always did, but the front door of the house was open as well. He got as far as the reception hall when Biti jumped up and brandished a big rock like a weapon.

"Biti!"

Biti dropped the rock, then stumbled forward and dropped to his knees in front of Ray. "My lord! I humbly apologize!"

Ray glanced around, but nothing looked out of place except for food platters and the remains of a dinner on one of the dining tables. "What happened?"

Biti moaned and held his head, prepared for a beating.

"Biti, tell me what happened," Ray said in as calm a voice as possible.

"My lord has been taken," Biti whispered, looking around as if someone might strike him at any moment. "The Medjay came. Your father has been taken."

Ray gasped. "Sermont was here?"

Biti nodded and ducked his head again, afraid that Ray might decide to beat him.

"Why? Did he say why he was here? Why did they take my father?"

Biti moaned. "They found things. Sacred objects. From tombs."

"Found them where?"

"Here! In the courtyard. Then they took my lord away. If he doesn't come back, my wife and I will be without a home. Our children will starve. And I will have to kill myself for my great failure to my lord," Biti said, planting his face against the ground. He wailed and threw sand in his hair.

"Biti, stop it!"

"I have failed! I have failed my lord!"

Bull appeared in the courtyard doorway and Ray beckoned him closer to get him off the street. When Biti saw Bull approaching, he wailed even more.

"Biti, tell me, did they take him to the jail?"

"Maybe. I don't know for sure! I was knocked out when they left." He shook his head, then looked up and grabbed Ray's arm. "But the old teacher may know! Khamenwati was here for the evening meal."

"Is he all right? Where was he when they took my father?"

"In the house. He didn't know! He heard nothing. I tried to explain what happened, but he has no patience for my kind. He was angry at being left alone. He called me a fool. I was afraid that he'd beat me. Me! The one who tried to defend my lord!"

"Biti, did Khamenwati say where he was going when he left?"

Biti looked down at the ground. "No, my lord. I'm sorry. I should have asked, but I didn't want to anger him more."

Bull bent over and gripped Biti's shoulders. Biti yelped, then calmed down as Bull lifted him to his feet and dusted him off. Ray watched in silence, wondering what Bull might be thinking.

"Okay," Bull said, staring into Biti's face and patting him on the shoulder. "Okay now."

Still trembling, Biti nodded.

Ray glanced at the open courtyard door, wondering if the police would return for him. "You did what you could, Biti. No one else is going to hurt you."

Ray looked at his reflection in the still water of the pond. With no one else available to watch Bull, he couldn't try to go after his father, even if he could come up with a clever plan to rescue him from Sermont, which seemed impossible. Of course, Mayor Paweraa had gotten Ray released in return for a gift from his father, so that was a possible solution, assuming Hapu was being held captive. In the meantime, he had to figure out how to hide Bull and keep him safe while he went off in search of his father.

A heavy hand clapped down on Ray's shoulder, startling him.

"Khamenwati," Bull said.

Ray thought about it a moment. "I suppose you're right, Bull. Good idea."

Bull smiled.

Startled by the sound of the red granite door quietly scraping on its hinges, Ray's head snapped around with the expectation of seeing Sermont with the rest of his thugs. What he actually saw in the brightening pre-dawn light surprised him even more —four priests with beards. And swords.

Without thinking, Ray grabbed Bull's arm and they ran around the far side of the pond toward the old tree that he had used as a child to sneak over the wall. The unexpected maneuver gave them a few precious seconds before the priests were able to follow on the other side of the pond. When they reached the tree, Bull needed no help, hauling himself up into its branches just as Ray started to climb. Ray gasped as a dagger thumped into the wood near his hand, prompting him to move faster. He heard the sound of running feet close behind.

Before Ray knew it, they were both up and over the wall.

#

When Khait first arrived in Thebes in the month of Phaophi, she marveled at how big and colorful everything looked from the river. Barges and boats of all kinds were tied up at the stone quays by the ancient city; some of them seagoing ships with foreign markings that plied their trade across the Great Green Sea. As the twenty watercraft in the retinue of Pharaoh Setnakhte approached the city, crowds swarmed along the east riverbank waiting to spot the pharaoh's massive cedar wood barge, the *Washi*, a grand demonstration of Egypt's power and wealth. The 195-foot-long barge held a curtained and spacious gold cabin in the middle decorated with golden rams' heads at each corner. Gold covered the sides of the barge down to the waterline. Blue and white flags snapped in the breeze. Despite the strong currents during the second month of flood season, the numerous sailors synchronized their oars with great precision to maneuver the barge toward the empty stone quay reserved for the pharaoh. Looming over the crowds, massive statues of pharaohs and gods gazed in defiance at the mortals below, standing as silent sentinels of eternity before their gleaming stone temples and bronze-tipped obelisks that flashed in the sunlight.

Beyond the riverbank crowds, broad processional avenues rain straight through the temple and administrative districts adjacent to the high-walled estates of the elite. In contrast to these organized spaces, narrower passages wound past the whitewashed mud-brick homes of the working class interspersed among the beer halls, marketplaces, warehouses, and lesser temples throughout the city. Khait thought the city looked exciting and intimidating. The clean lines of the temple district felt familiar and comfortable, much like the smaller and newer city of Pi-Ramesses with its grid of wide avenues and canals. However, Thebes was ancient and larger than her childhood home of Heliopolis, presenting itself as a noisy chaos of people, animals, odors, and bright colors. As they approached the quay, maneuvering around the papyrus and floating weeds that jutted into the river from marshy sections of the east bank, the sounds of music, voices, and shrieking children hesitated and resolved into a building wave of cheers and rhythmic chants to welcome Pharaoh Setnakhte. With the pharaoh's arrival, the people would feel secure and the annual festival could truly begin.

Six days after her arrival in Thebes, exhausted from her duties to the royal family during the first part of the Opet Festival, Khait ate her breakfast of bread and beer and journeyed across the Nile to the west bank on one of the royal boats. She was now in the land of the dead, crowded with enormous statues of long-dead kings, obelisks and stelae filled with history, towering mortuary temples, sem-priests from the House of Beauty ready to sell funeral wares and books of the dead to grieving families, shaded food and drink stands where offerings could be purchased for the gods or for family tombs, and wide processional avenues leading from the major temples to the river. High white walls surrounded many of the temple estates with their hives of buildings dominated by the vast barrel-vaulted warehouses that held the empire's granaries, cattle, ivory, minerals, and metals. Shaded courtyards beside the warehouses were occupied by the scribes who counted, organized, and distributed this great wealth. The Opet Festival was still going strong, so occasional snatches of music and singing drifted across the river from the east side, but Khait was happy to get away from the crowds to this quieter ancient necropolis.

After stopping for a jar of beer at a food stand, Khait asked for directions and eventually found her way to the head of the valley where 300-foot vertical sandstone cliffs towered over *Djeser-djeseru*, the mortuary temple of the female Pharaoh Hatshepsut. Facing east, the temple glowed with power in the clear early morning light. As with other mortuary temples, this "mansion of millions of years" was separate from Hatshepsut's tomb in the Valley of the Kings, serving to commemorate the pharaoh's reign with historical wall paintings, inscriptions, and statues, but also providing a place for the living to commune with the dead pharaoh. The temple sat at the base of a natural bowl formed by the cliffs and seemed to grow out of the rock in the long, clean lines of three stepped terraces, each held aloft by a double row of 100-foot-tall columns. Built over 250 years earlier, it was certainly one of the largest temples Khait had ever seen and had been dedicated to Amun, but it also contained the sanctuary of Hathor, goddess and protector of the Theban necropolis. The terraces were connected by long limestone ramps leading down to the valley floor where a wide causeway was lined with sphinxes and surrounded by fragrant gardens full of frankincense and myrrh trees.

When Khait reached the second level, she saw Hathor's sanctuary at the southern end of the colonnade. Passing into the sanctuary's hypostyle hall, where twelve round columns topped with images of Hathor supported the roof high overhead, Khait stopped to admire the room. Wall paintings depicted Hatshepsut dancing, drinking milk from Hathor in her cow form, or sitting between Hathor and Amun. At this early hour of the morning, sunlight slanted across the columns to make the paintings come alive. Continuing down the central aisle to the holy-of-holies, Khait bowed low and cautiously entered the dimly lit home of Hathor, where slender columns topped with Hathor images supported the vaulted roof of the smaller chamber. The roof was painted dark blue with yellow stars. This end of the building had been carved out of the mountain and finished with rock slabs that were then decorated with brightly painted relief sculpture.

Alone in the deep silence and shadows of the sanctuary, Khait laid down on her stomach with her arms outstretched toward Hathor's golden shrine. It seemed odd that there were no priests here to protect the goddess, accept offerings, or keep the purifying incense burning, but she thought she felt the presence of the goddess behind the heavy curtains woven with gold thread. She felt the motherly protection of the gentle goddess and it calmed her mind.

Khait jumped as she heard footsteps.

"What are you doing?" It was a woman's voice. "Get up."

Confused, Khait got to her feet. "But...I don't want to disrespect the goddess," she said, gesturing toward the closed curtains of the shrine.

The frowning old woman had to be in her fifties. She wore the pleated white robes of a temple priestess with the addition of a leopard skin draped over one shoulder. Her head was bald and she probably bathed four times a day. Studying Khait's face with her intense brown eyes, she raised one kohled eyebrow. "The goddess is not here. Her honored presence attends the Opet Festival to visit with the other gods in celebration. Are you lost?"

"No, Mistress. I apologize. I was told to come here by her Great Majesty, Queen Isis."

The old woman gasped. "Queen Isis sent you? Why?"

"I am to meet with the High Priestess Shepsit."

"I see. Then someone should have told you to look for me in the temple's administrative district, which is below us on the valley floor."

It dawned on Khait that she had found Shepsit. "I'm sorry, Mistress. I didn't think of that."

Shepsit stepped back through the shrine's portal and beckoned Khait to follow. As Khait emerged into the brighter light of the hypostyle hall, Shepsit carefully studied Khait's clothing, her jewelry, and what she could see of her body through the transparent white linen. "I was told someone would be coming. Are you here to learn the mysteries of Hathor's temple?"

"I am honored to be that person, Mistress."

Shepsit nodded and gestured with her hand. "Rotate."

Khait slowly turned in a circle.

"Can you sing without scaring children?"

Yes, Mistress."

"Can you dance gracefully without falling over?"

"Yes, Mistress."

Shepsit nodded. "That's a start. You'd be amazed how clumsy some of the young women are that they send me."

Khait noticed that one of Shepsit's front teeth was missing. Not unusual for someone of her advanced age, but distracting.

"Well, if you're only here for a month, we better get started. We have a long walk, but we can take the back way and introduce you to the first of the mysteries."

"I would be honored, Mistress."

"Of course you would," said Shepsit, gesturing for her to follow as she re-entered the sanctuary of Hathor.

Khait hesitated, confused again.

Shepsit's head poked around the corner of the portal. "I should have asked if you can follow simple instructions. Can you?"

Khait nodded and stepped through the portal. When she

was inside, it took a moment before her eyes adjusted and she realized that Shepsit was gone. "Mistress?"

Khait heard a heavy sigh from behind the curtained shrine of the goddess, followed by Shepsit's echoing voice some distance away. "I worry that Queen Isis has sent me a simpleton. Behind the sanctuary, child. Walk around it and look down."

Feeling like a child, Khait stepped around the shrine and saw steps descending into a hole cut into the rock floor. Candles burned in niches. The circular stairwell was wide, but Khait was able to brace herself against the walls with her outstretched arms. Far below, Shepsit was looking up at her with a grim expression. Khait wasn't normally disturbed by heights or tight spaces, but the deep shadows far below Shepsit were disconcerting.

"This is the first mystery, child. This is how we channel the words of the goddess and speak to those who bring offerings and ask questions of the oracle. Now, if can remember how to walk, follow me and I'll take you to your new home away from home."

#

Neferabu had the hands and the talent of a master painter—and he knew it. Although he had been banned from sculpture in the tombs and forced to work in what he considered to be the secondary medium of daubing paint on rock, he had the touch of greatness. He was Neferabu, son of Neferabu, of the Gang that Works on the Right, so the workers of the Great Place knew from the time of his birth that he would have the artistic skills of his famous ancestors. After years of practicing the proper techniques of chiseling and polishing stone, his talent took over and he began to create his art in an unorthodox style that had brought only stares of disapproval from the other workers—and his father. Perhaps a full-face portrait rather than a profile was chiseled into the stone, or the legs of a figure weren't turned sideways in the standard pose. Eventually, he was banned from carving the limestone and forced to take up the brush and paint pots. He also excelled at that, of course, and as the workers of the royal tombs created their own monuments to the afterlife, many of them contacted Neferabu because they knew he was the best. Due to his fame, and the higher price of his private work, the single women of the village—and even some of the attached women—were drawn to him as bees were drawn to a brightly colored flower.

Inside the royal tombs, the quarrymen would cut precise tunnels or chambers and flatten their walls, then the plasterers would create a smooth white surface for the artists. An even grid of lines would be formed by snapping a paint-dipped string against the plaster. Within the squares of the grid, an outline artist such as Neferabu would wield his brush straight out from his shoulder, moving his arm in precise brush strokes and lines to create lifelike figures of gods and kings where none had been before. Indeed, Neferabu felt the power of Amun-Re, king of the gods, directing the motions of his arm in the act of creation. Scenes from the daily life of a dead pharaoh became complete stories of a virtuous life under Neferabu's skilled hands. Ritual phrases came to life as the black paint became hieroglyphs. Sculptors would then give depth to the outlined images on the walls by carving them out of the plaster in relief. With any luck, they wouldn't ruin Neferabu's work. On large tomb projects, the coloring artists would then fill in the outlines and details of each figure, otherwise the outline artist would do his own coloring.

Neferabu preferred to do his own painting when he could, not trusting the hesitant brush strokes of the less-talented coloring artists. His clean outlines that gave life to the gods could be demolished in an instant by the haphazard paint splashing of amateurs.

In fact, the paint itself became one of Neferabu's tools. After learning the simpler techniques of paint mixing from the coloring artists, he began to experiment until he learned the secrets of the pigments. Each color had its own personality, but Neferabu was able to give his paints an iridescent glow that sparkled like polished gemstones to animate the gods—even in the dim light of the inner tomb chambers where they would be most important to the pharaohs crossing the western horizon. Of course, he also would have preferred to do his own relief carving of the figures, but the sculptors were strong and feared for their livelihoods, refusing to be outdone by a young upstart who would not follow the conventional rules of their craft. Neferabu might have found this easier to tolerate if his own father were not among the sculptors who kept him away from the stone.

However, in his own home, which also served as his private workshop, he could paint whatever he wanted. He also secretly sculpted small *ushabti* tomb figures and other works for people in his community who wished to have the best for their personal tombs in the village cemetery. Most of them only worked one day out of every four, and their wages were supplied in grain and other supplies from the royal storehouses, so much of their spare time was spent on digging and building the private houses of death that would house them for eternity. While they might not live in the large homes of nobles or the wealthy officials of the city, they were the privileged workers of the Great Place, and their journeys into the afterlife would benefit from the decorations and furnishings that they could supply for their own beautiful tombs.

In the front room of his home in the tomb workers' village, Neferabu's taste for striking colors was immediately made apparent to the visitor. The ceiling here, as in the rest of the house, was painted in the brilliant Egyptian blue that looked like the calm waters of the eternal Nile before flood season. This was the hardest of the paint colors to make, requiring a long process of heating a special mixture of glittering sand, copper filings, and the same natron that was used for cleaning and for drying out corpses for mummification. The ceiling was supported by reddish-brown columns, the tops of the walls held a border of blue lotus petals on a green background above a red band, and the whitewashed walls had been filled with murals of pleasant hunting and farming scenes. The original floor had been covered with unglazed tiles, and these were painted in patterns of red, yellow, and white, although it was now spotted with other bright colors because he also used this room as his workshop.

At the moment, his workshop also held two unusual decorations that lent a youthful energy to the room—the eligible daughters of Foreman Paneb of the Gang that Works on the Left. One of them was tall and ephemeral Hatia, the subject of his current work in red granite, and the other was Heria, her younger sister, who was shorter with a curvier figure. When they had arrived early that morning, they had both been dressed in the simple white work dresses they wore when carrying water to their house or preparing food, but these simple garments had quickly been discarded after their arrival. Fascinated by Nefer-abu, they often visited him in the morning when they were able to sneak away from their chores. By offering special services to the famous artist, they were able to pay for small statues of themselves in red granite, allowing them to spend more time with him while holding his complete attention. Conveniently, Neferabu was also fascinated by the two of them, so he worked more slowly and charged more for his work than he would have under normal circumstances. In the near future, preferably before Foreman Paneb learned of the attentions showered on the artist by his daughters, Neferabu planned to make them the first of his wives that he would gather for his harem, which he could now afford to support with his new wealth. He planned to have many wives, of many sizes, shapes, skills, and interests, who would all work together to bring him great happiness and many children. He would need a larger house, of course, perhaps in one of the wealthier districts of Thebes, but he would soon be able to afford such a luxury as he and Khenti continued looting the royal tomb they had found. The Greek trader paid well for their efforts, but even if he didn't return, there would be others ready to buy their treasures. In the meantime, he and Khenti had only to maintain a low profile, continuing with their regular jobs and staying in their regular surroundings until they were ready to leave the village entirely.

Neferabu was focused on the task of etching Hatia's face out of the granite with his sharp bronze detail chisel when he heard a crunch of gravel at his front doorstep. When he turned, fear-ing that he might discover the hulking form of Paneb blocking the exit, he was relieved to see the young Ruta standing in the doorway instead, his hands shining with a gold or silver ring on each of his fingers.

"Come in, Ruta."

Ruta glanced at Hatia and Heria, who giggled when they saw him. Ruta quickly looked away and nodded at Neferabu.

"Sorry to disturb, master."

"That's all right, Ruta. You're not interrupting." He leaned in closer to whisper in the boy's ear. "However, I would like to caution you to wear fewer rings on your hands when you're out in public. No one is used to seeing them on you, so you might draw too much attention. You understand?" He glanced at Hatia and Heria to reassure himself that they had no idea of what he was talking about with the boy. Hatia continued holding her pose, apparently not listening, while Heria looked at him with a coy expression and ran her tongue over a date she held between two fingers.

Ruta nodded and waggled his fingers so that the rings would catch the light. "Shiny."

"Yes. Very shiny. That's the problem. You should keep them hidden safely away—at least for a little while."

"I understand, master."

"Good. So what brings you here this morning?"

"Khenti said to bring a message."

Neferabu felt a cold tingle in his stomach. "Yes? What is it?"

"He accepts your offer," Ruta said, glancing at the women again. "You should meet him tonight."

Neferabu sighed, wondering why Khenti had changed his mind. He really had no interest in crawling around in tight tunnels deep beneath the earth, eating dust and fighting for air.

It wasn't natural. A man of his talents shouldn't risk his life, or even his agile hands, in such activities. He had only offered his help because he knew that Khenti would say no. Still, he supposed that if he were there to motivate Khenti to keep looting the tomb, it would all be worthwhile.

Neferabu glanced at the two women, studying their aesthetically pleasing forms for a long moment and thinking about the simple pleasures in life, before he finally sighed again and nodded at Ruta. "Okay. Tell him I'll be there."

#

Ray banged his fist against the old door, shaking flakes of red paint from the wood. Khamenwati's house was adjacent to the Theban school for scribes in the Temple of Amun-Re, so there were plenty of priests in the neighborhood despite the early hour. Student scribes and future tomb artists milled about in the alleys waiting for their tutors to summon them inside, using the time by either writing on the walls or drawing on them according to their training. These were the best-looking alleys in the entire city of Thebes.

A muffled voice yelled through the door. "Who dares to summon the wise Khamenwati from his bed at this early hour? If you're not the great god Thoth come to earth to speak with me, then prepare for your journey to meet Osiris!"

"Khamenwati," Ray yelled. "Let us in! I'm Ray, son of Hapu, and I'm here with my friend!"

"Come back later! I'm busy!"

Ray banged on the door again. "Please, my lord! My father is in danger! We need your help!"

The door opened a crack and Khamenwati peeked outside. "You need my help? What do you mean?"

"Can I tell you inside? Please?"

Khamenwati studied Bull, then Ray, then reluctantly opened the door and stepped aside to let them in, leaning on his ivory cane.

Ray started to speak, but Khamenwati motioned for silence, then gestured at the ugly dwarf god, Bes, standing in his niche shrine in the side wall. Not wanting to show disrespect to the protector of the household, Ray kept his mouth shut as he and Bull followed Khamenwati up the steps into the small reception room. After their run across the city, Ray's heavy breathing was loud in the quiet confines of the house.

The only furniture was the single chair on the dais, but there were plenty of mats scattered on the floor. Stacks of rolled papyrus books and stone *ostraca* covered in the fine black markings of hieratic script rested on the dais beside the chair. Paintings of the great god Thoth, with the long black beak of his bird head turned in profile atop a man's body, dominated the room along with large blocks of hieroglyphs telling the story of how Thoth had given language and writing to the people of the Two Lands. The flickering light of the oil lamps allowed enough light to read by before the stronger light of the sun-boat rose to illuminate everything through the high windows that faced east.

"Speak," Khamenwati said, sitting down heavily in his chair as he munched on a loaf of bread.

Ray quickly told the story of how they had arrived at Hapu's house after his arrest, followed by their discovery by murderous priests. He didn't explain why priests would be trying to kill them.

"What have you done?"

"I'm sorry, my lord. I don't understand the question."

Khamenwati gestured at Bull with the bread loaf in his left hand, then changed the subject. "This friend of yours. Big fellow, isn't he? A boy his size on a farm would have much darker skin from being outside so much. Probably as strong as a hippo. Who is he?"

"Well, we call him Bull," Ray said, wondering if Hapu had told him anything about their situation. "He's a student scribe, so he doesn't get out much."

"Interesting. A common nickname for an uncommon young fellow. Does he speak?"

"Sometimes," Ray said. "He's simple."

"I'm simple," Bull said, eyeing the loaf of bread in Khamenwati's hand. "And I'm hungry."

Khamenwati tore off a hunk of bread from the loaf and tossed it to Bull, who quickly stuffed it into his mouth. "I can see he's got the evil spirits inside. You have to be careful with his sort. Not dangerous, is he?"

"Not at all," Ray said.

"Not at all," Bull said through his mouth full of bread.

"You like the bread, Bull? You want some more?" Khamenwati asked, breaking off another chunk from the loaf.

Bull nodded.

"Then tell me something. Your nickname is Bull, but what's your real name? What do your parents call you?"

Before Ray could stop him, Bull replied, "Bull."

Ray relaxed.

"Or Ramesses," Bull said.

Khamenwati looked at Ray, who licked his lips and wondered how he could explain this away. The old scribe couldn't be fooled.

"Ramesses, you say. And Ray is your friend?"

Bull nodded and caught the bread that Khamenwati tossed to him.

"And your father, his name is also Ramesses?"

"Yes," Bull said, biting into the bread.

Ray rubbed his face with his hands, fearing what would happen next. There were only two ways this could go. Either Khamenwati was their friend, or he would turn them over to the Medjay. Either way, he now knew who they really were, and that was dangerous.

Despite what he was hearing, Khamenwati's voice remained calm. "Then I begin to see why these so-called priests might be chasing you, and perhaps even why Hapu has been arrested. Tell me no more about this young man," he said, nodding at Bull. "As you are now a guest in my house, you should know that I will protect you as much as I can."

Ray bowed deeply. "We are honored, my lord. My father has often commented on your wisdom and generosity, and it's clear that the great Amun-Re is watching over us by bringing us here to your home. We thank you for any help you may give us."

"And you're wondering what to do about Hapu, I assume."

"Yes, my lord."

"I was there when they took him, you know. His foolish servants left me sitting at the dinner table wondering where Hapu had gone. If I'd known that he was being kidnapped, I would have defended him with all of my ability," Khamenwati said, shaking his ivory cane.

"Of course, my lord."

Khamenwati thumped the end of his cane against the floor. "Back in my day, we had more control over the Medjay. Now, these ruffians think they own the city. A man can't eat in his own house without some Medjay captain barging in to interrupt his meal. It's a sad state of affairs."

"Indeed," Ray said.

"Now, the whole system is corrupt, as if the gods can't see what these men are doing. The world is out of balance. Grain goes missing from the royal granaries. Precious objects are stolen from tombs. And decent scribes get arrested for upsetting city officials. The vizier tries to maintain control, but he is only one man. Such is the way of things."

Ray noticed that Bull had found another loaf of bread, which he was now eating. "My lord, how can we get my father released? I have nothing to trade for him but myself. Sermont might accept such an exchange."

Khamenwati rapped his cane against the dais again. "A fool's bargain. Something has happened to focus their attention on Hapu. They won't let him go easily, if at all."

"There must be something we can do."

Khamenwati looked up at the large wall painting of Thoth. "There is, but I'll need some time to think."

Two

1184 BCE—Royal City of Pi-Ramesses

Year 4 of His Majesty, King of Upper and Lower Egypt, Chosen by Re, Beloved of Amun, Pharaoh Setnakhte, Second Month of Akhet (Season of Inundation), Day 21

#

In the royal city of Pi-Ramesses, two living gods occupied the golden house.

To the dismay of Ramesses III, the boats had returned from the Beautiful Feast of Opet with the news that his father, Setnakhte, was very ill. The old pharaoh had insisted that he be allowed to celebrate the ritual in Thebes, knowing that he might be doing so for the last time. Seini, the royal physician, had accompanied him on the trip, and he had been joined by others from the Theban House of Life for the return journey. Despite all of the attention from the assembled priests, the spells, potions, and prayers of their healing arts had done little to slow the old pharaoh's gradual decay. Ramesses had watched as High Priest Bakenkhons descended from the royal boat, making him wonder if perhaps the rivalry between the priesthood and the pharaohs might have escalated during the return trip from Thebes. It was certainly possible that Bakenkhons could have arranged to poison Setnakhte or weaken him with magic spells. However, Ramesses suspected it was more likely that Setnakhte felt responsible for the death of Amana and the disappearance of Bull. Due to his long absence from the palace, Ramesses felt his own guilt at not being able to defend his son, and this was mixed with the natural sadness of Amana's journey to meet Osiris. Because of this attack by cowardly assassins, Meryey and the rest of the Tjehenu tribes would be swept from the face of the earth by the mighty arm of Ramesses, unleashed in terrible vengeance like the desert wind that shreds skin from bone. Their men would be cut down and crushed by the army of Pharaoh; their women and children captured and put to work as slaves. But that would have to wait. For now, he had to wait for news while Didu hunted for Bull, Ray, and Hapu—only then could he learn the truth behind the murder of Amana.

The inside of Setnakhte's bedchamber was as cool as a tomb dug deep into the earth. When Ramesses entered, Queen Teya was feeding bits of fish and dates to the old pharaoh, even though he didn't appear to be enjoying it, trying to turn his head away whenever her hand approached his mouth. She gasped and sat back on the edge of the low bed when she realized that Ramesses had entered the room.

"Did I startle you, Teya?"

Teya lowered her head and briefly stretched out her arms. "I am always delighted to be in the presence of my lord. You are like the life-giving rays of the solar disk lighting up the room."

"We know that Amun-Re loves us because he allows us to bask in your light," added a male voice in the shadows.

Ramesses studied the bowing dark shape near the wall and recognized Pentawere. He thought it odd that he hadn't recognized Pen's voice. The boy surprised him sometimes with his ability to remain hidden in plain view within a room.

"Pentawere," Ramesses said. "It's good that you are here helping your mother."

"Oh, yes, he's a great help," Teya said. "As always."

Ramesses knelt by the bed and looked into Setnakhte's face. The good god's eyes were closed. His breathing was shallow and his breath smelled of fish and dates. "Father?"

Setnakhte's eyes opened halfway. His mouth formed a word, but no sound came out of it.

"He is unable to speak," Teya said, rubbing Setnakhte's chest. "The evil spirits are stealing his breath."

"Where is the physician?"

"Seini and the others have gone outside to discuss his condition. They didn't want to upset the good god while they were arguing about what treatments they should use to restore his breath and his voice."

"If I may, I'll go and check on them," Pen said, taking a step forward and waiting for approval. Ramesses nodded and he left the room.

It was unfortunate that Setnakhte couldn't discuss the situation with him. After Pasai's arrest and the other events that followed the return of Ramesses to Pi-Ramesses, and with Setnakhte's lengthy journey to Thebes, there had been no opportunity to hear his father's ideas about the kidnapping and other evils that had invaded the golden house. His arm of justice was Didu, who might only now be reaching Thebes to look for answers, so there were no current reports to act on as yet. The queens were able to shed little light on events during the night of the assassins because everyone had been at the Festival of Drunkenness. The palace guards on that night were no longer among the living—either killed by assassins or executed for their failures—so they could not be interrogated. General Hori was ready to set out with the army once more to destroy the remnants of the Tjehenu tribes, including the Libu and the Meshwesh, but Ramesses still counseled patience. He had to know Setnakhte's thoughts.

In addition, if the time had come for his father to journey over the western horizon, there would be much to do that would require the attendance of Ramesses at the golden house and in the Great Place at Thebes. Orders had already been issued for construction on Setnakhte's intended tomb to be halted because it would take many more years before it would be ready for use. In fact, Setnakhte's tomb workers had recently run into the old tomb of Pharaoh Amenmesse during their fourth year of construction, prompting repairs to that tomb, and it still needed to be ritually sealed by the priests of the necropolis when the repairs were complete. The rest of Setnakhte's tomb workers had been reassigned to alter an older tomb formerly occupied by Queen Twosret. She was the last pharaoh of the previous dynasty, and her two-year reign had ended in a civil war lasting many years before Setnakhte, and eventually Ramesses III himself, brought order back to the Two Lands. Twosret's mummy had been relocated to a place of less honor because of her connection with the great enemy Bay, who had started the civil war. Twosret's sarcophagus was now being repainted for his own son, Amana, and her tomb was being modified for Setnakhte. Such was the way of the Great Place. Time continued without end, pharaohs continued to die, and tombs continued to resurface for new occupants under the shifting political sands of practicality.

Teya touched his arm, disturbing his thoughts.

"Yes?"

"I've not seen your great mother, Tiymerenese, around for some time. Should she not be by her husband's side during these dark hours? The other women of the harem have visited, but I've sent them all away."

"My mother is in her own apartments recovering from the flux. I think the trip to Thebes was too strenuous for both of them." He watched as Teya rinsed the fish oil from her fingers in a bowl of water. "Speaking of the missing, where is Pepi?"

"He tasted the god's food before I brought it in from the kitchen. He annoys me with his stupid questions, so I told him to stay out until I was through in here."

"Setnakhte likes him. That should be his decision."

Teya sighed and gestured at the sleeping pharaoh. "Look at him. He communes with the gods. He decides nothing right now."

Ramesses nodded. "You speak the truth, and I'm sure he appreciates your feeding him. He has always liked you. However, please leave us now. I wish to have some private time with him."

Teya bowed and stood up with the food bowl. "As you wish, my lord. I'll be outside. Call for me if you need me."

"I will."

Ramesses watched Teya leave. Her diaphanous gown fluttered around her as she walked quietly away on bare feet. She was a good wife, if somewhat prone to mischief, and had raised their son, Pentawere, in the proper fashion befitting a prince who might one day rule the Two Lands.

"She's gone?" Setnakhte whispered.

Surprised, Ramesses turned his head to study his father. "Teya has left. Are you still hungry?"

Setnakhte frowned and gave one violent shake of his head. "Nothing tastes good."

Ramesses leaned closer so that he could hear better. Setnakhte's whispers sounded like they were coming from the afterlife. "She said you couldn't talk."

Setnakhte took a slow, deep breath. "Better that way. Few words left. Enemies everywhere."

"Everywhere? What do you mean?"

Setnakhte tried to lift his arm, but it was too heavy, so he decided to roll his eyes around in a slow circle. "Here."

Ramesses stiffened. "Who?"

"Not sure. Find Pasai. He may know."

"We have Pasai," Ramesses said, his stomach feeling hollow at the thought of Pasai's betrayal. "He's in the jail pit. He helped the assassins. I should execute him, but I want more proof first."

Setnakhte frowned. "No. Not possible."

"Pentawere knows the truth."

"You spoke to Pasai?"

"I won't listen to his lies. Pentawere and General Hori interrogated him, but he wouldn't confess. As I ordered, Hori stopped the questioning when they reached the point where a man lies to save himself."

Setnakhte broke into a coughing fit, then settled back again in exhaustion. Ramesses offered him a cup of water, but the old pharaoh was barely conscious now.

"I'll let you rest, Father. May the blood of the gods renew itself within you, giving you health for a full 110 years on this earth."

As Ramesses stood up, Setnakhte jerked his arm and whispered, "Find the boy. Bring to me."

Ramesses sighed. "I've sent people to hunt for young Bull. They haven't had any luck so far, but he may be in Thebes."

"No." Setnakhte jerked his head. "Priest. With Bakenkhons." After a brief coughing fit, Setnakhte closed his eyes and Ramesses bent down to hear the last word. "Itennu."

#

Despite the fact that he spent so much time painting the walls in dimly lighted tunnels and chambers of royal tombs, Neferabu didn't like tight spaces. When he had offered to help Khenti steal tomb objects, he never thought Khenti would actually take him up on his offer, although he put on a good show of really wanting to help the quarryman empty the burial chamber he had discovered. Trapped by his own maneuvering of his friend, Neferabu now found himself in a deep, dark hole in the ground, under rock that would crush him if Khenti's digging somehow caused it to cave in. Breathing was difficult, not only because of the dust disturbed by their activities, but also from a limited air supply and the smoky soot generated by their two torches. If he didn't have such a strong desire to be rich, he never would have forced himself to crawl down the long and narrow tunnel, across pointed chunks of limestone and the occasional black scorpion, to reach the eternal home of the dead noble and his wife.

Once he was in the burial chamber itself, Neferabu was able to stand in a crouch and admire the logical and industrious manner in which Khenti had removed the tomb objects so far. The gold had been removed first, of course, because it was the easiest to melt down to disguise its place of origin. Silver and electrum objects followed, also to be melted down, after which came the precious oils, ointments, and spices that could be transferred to new containers to disguise them. So that they wouldn't have to worry about discarding marked containers from the burial chamber, some of these transfers occurred while Khenti and Ruta worked inside the tomb so that they could leave the original containers in the chamber.

On this trip, Khenti and Neferabu were taking the time to crawl through a second passage into a storage chamber that had been looted once before, probably by the priests or other members of the original burial party. Khenti said he'd heard rumors of that happening on occasion. However, the original robbers had left a few containers of exotic oils, some non-perishable cosmetics, and piles of costly fine linens that Khenti and Neferabu were able to remove, passing them up into the narrow tunnel where Ruta waited to ferry them to the surface for transport on the sled.

Back in the burial chamber, they studied the objects crammed into the room that were far too large for them to drag through the tunnel. Khenti had already peeled off the gold leaf and other decorations where he could, but Neferabu was able to help him move some of the cabinets and other heavy furniture so that Khenti could remove more of the gold and silver.

Down to the last of the small objects, they turned to the mummy cases themselves, which didn't seem all that promising due to the work of the original tomb robbers. In this case, the outermost sarcophagus of the nested set that contained one of the mummies, a woman named Tuyu, looked as perfect as the day it had been buried, complete with the seals of the necropolis priests of Osiris. However, once Khenti and Neferabu had removed the outermost lid of the sarcophagus, which had been too heavy for Khenti and Ruta to lift, they discovered that the gold mask and other gilded objects on the inner coffin had been removed before the burial. Guests at the funeral would never have suspected that anything was missing. Maneuvering in the cramped space was difficult, so once they saw that the seals on the inner coffin had been broken, they didn't bother to continue.

The next sarcophagus, belonging to a man named Yuya—one of Pharaoh Amenhotep III's in-laws and the great grandfather of Pharaoh Tutankhamun—was in similar condition. The gold had been removed from the inner coffin's surfaces, but this time the seals were intact. Knowing that the burial officials might also have sealed it after ransacking the mummy for its jewelry and other ceremonial objects, they were surprised when they lifted the lid to discover valuable objects on top of the outer linen wrappings. The mummy had been sealed with a black resinous pitch, but the embalmers hadn't done a thorough job, leaving areas of the linen wrapping exposed. The large items were a gold embalming plate and a golden hawk pectoral with spread wings that was embedded with a variety of blue and green stones.

Smiling, Neferabu watched Khenti place the objects in a reed basket for Ruta to take to the surface. "Do you have anything to cut the wrappings, Khenti? I want to go deeper."

Khenti frowned at him. "I don't want to disturb the mummy. We might anger the spirit *ka*."

"You got me to come all the way down here into this hole. I want to make sure we don't have to come back again."

"Nef, we've done very well. We both have enough to live like kings. There's no need to come back."

Neferabu looked down at the small pile of weapons near his feet, which they had ignored up to this point. He reached down and picked up a short, curved sword that would easily slice through the wrappings.

"Put it down," Khenti said. "The *ka*!"

Neferabu sighed. "The *ka*, the *ka*! You sound like an old woman."

Khenti handed the basket to Ruta, then prepared to climb up into the tunnel after it. "If you want more, you'll have to get it without my help."

"Fine. Just don't try to cheat me out of what we've gathered tonight. I remember everything."

With an angry growl, Khenti placed his torch in the tunnel near his head, pulled himself up, and began scrambling across the limestone chips on his way to the surface.

Neferabu quickly cut through the mummy wrappings around the hands, revealing gold finger stalls, six gold rings, and a bracelet. He put these new items into the remaining reed basket and started to leave when he noticed a gilded scarab and a gold staff of office shoved into a narrow crevice between the larger sarcophagus and the wall. The scarab went straight into the reed basket, but the staff was too large, so he tucked it under his arm and started toward the tunnel opening when he noticed the gold yoke on the chariot. Obviously, the chariot was too large to fit through the small tunnel, but there were other heavy objects in the burial chamber that could be used to break the yoke and free the gold. A tall statue of Anubis stood directly beside it, but he wasn't going to take the chance of angering the god, so something else would have to serve. He finally resorted to kneeling beside the stone sarcophagus lid that had conveniently not landed flat on the rocky floor, ducking under it so that he could use the muscles in his legs to lift it, and flipped it over onto the chariot, which smashed nicely under the weight of the heavy stone lid. The gold yoke was free now, but still too wide for the tunnel. If he tried to make a fire to melt it, or took the time to break it up more, it would be morning before he finally crawled out of the tunnel on the surface, so he finally gave up.

Wondering if Khenti and Ruta would be waiting for him, he slowly dragged himself through the tunnel, pushing his torch well ahead of him, followed by the reed basket full of treasure. The gradual climb in the narrow space seemed to take forever, but he focused on the fire ahead of him and used his fear of the tight space to keep his tired muscles working as quickly as they could.

His first breath of air from the surface tasted sweet, reminding him of how much he enjoyed life. There were so many things he could do now, so many choices, that it would take him weeks to figure out what he wanted to do next. He could travel in style, buy nice places to live, collect beautiful women for his harem, have dozens of children, and the wealth would last forever. Life had never been so good.

Ruta lifted the torch from the entrance and ground it into the sand to put it out. The golden sun-boat was just below the eastern horizon.

"Hurry, master!"

Neferabu pushed his reed basket of loot out of the tunnel and dragged himself out onto the sand and rocks, thinking how pleasant they felt on his skin, when he noticed that Khenti had left with the sled.

"Where's Khenti?"

"He left. Long time ago. He said we could catch him."

Neferabu sighed heavily, thinking about his sore muscles as he realized he'd have to carry the heavy reed basket and the gold staff all the way down to their hiding place at the river by himself. He reached into the basket and gave the rings to Ruta. "Here. These are for you."

Ruta smiled and immediately put the rings on his fingers. "Shiny!"

"And there's more if you'll carry this basket as long as you can. This gold staff is heavy."

"Yes, yes," Ruta said, hefting the basket. "I'll carry. Thank you, master."

They started down into a narrow ravine that would save them some time in descending the hill. The sled hadn't been able to travel that way, but if they walked fast, they might actually catch Khenti before he reached the hiding place. Not too fast, of course, because Neferabu was already tired and didn't want to unload heavy objects from the basket if he could avoid it.

As they neared the mouth of the ravine, Neferabu stepped into the softer sand of a wash and heard a sound that almost made his heart stop. Chariots. Moving fast.

Without thinking, Neferabu shoved Ruta and his basket into a shadowy depression behind a big boulder in the ravine. Ruta was startled, but the look in his eyes told Neferabu that he'd heard the same ominous sounds approaching. The gold scarab fell out of the basket, so Neferabu picked it up. The boulder wasn't large enough to hide both of them, so with the scarab in his left hand and the staff in his right, Neferabu started sprinting across the wash to a shadowy ravine on the other side. The rapid clatter of chariot wheels on rocks echoed through the shallow main canyon like thunder.

A bolt of fire in Neferabu's thigh made him think he'd pulled a muscle, but when he glanced down he saw an arrow.

The second arrow hit him in his right side and knocked him down.

#

The House of Beauty was always busy. The funeral rite was generally considered to be the most important ceremony in a person's life, preparing the deceased for immortality in the beautiful Field of Reeds, so the preparation of the body and the ritual of purification had to be done right. The stakes were high—the spirit could survive in the kingdom of Osiris only as long as the discarded earthly body survived. The loss of the physical body, whether through natural decay or destruction, usually meant that the deceased would meet the dreaded Second Death, from which there would be no return. Soldiers on the battlefield were an exception, but their names would be recorded where they were buried so that the gods would be able to find them. Pharaohs and other wealthy nobles also took the precaution of having statues of themselves made so that the spirit had a refuge in the event of the body's destruction. Of course, not everyone could afford lavish ceremonies or statues, but even the lower levels of the working class joined mortuary cults to share the expenses of proper rituals.

As Itennu had seen, the process was always the same. A body would arrive with a family member or two, price and features of the mummification and funeral would be negotiated, Bai or one of the other sleazy negotiators would steal valuables from the body, and the mummification process would begin, taking over two months to complete by the time the corpse had been *osirified* for eternity and the all-day funeral took place. On rare occasions, however, a royal corpse would arrive and the management would descend on the common wetyu to make sure proper procedures were followed and that the corpse was not harmed or stripped of its valuables prior to the funeral. According to Itennu's ancient mentor, Ay, it was still possible in some cases for the funeral team to steal valuables from the sarcophagus before the necropolis priests applied the proper tomb seals, but it was a risky move that could lead to execution. For the most part, workers in the House of Beauty looked out for each other and lied to the managing sem-priests when necessary, knowing that they themselves could meet with untimely accidents if they broke the code of silence. Ay had also worked there long enough to know that the necropolis priests were not above the subtle looting of new tombs themselves, picking up a trinket or two to ensure that they would lead lives of comfort in their old age, but such opportunities were rare.

Itennu learned all of these details when the body of Prince Amanakhopshaf, the brother of Ramesses IV, arrived at the House of Beauty in Thebes. Before he even knew the identity of the new arrival, Itennu became aware of a rush of activity in the Place of Purification, led by Setau himself as Overseer of the Mysteries and First Prophet of Osiris in Thebes. When Setau placed the terracotta dog head of Anubis over his own head and his assistants escorted him outside—because he couldn't see well enough through the mask's eye holes to walk far by himself— Itennu knew something unusual was happening. At the time, he was standing in for Ay by burying a corpse in the white cleansing powder known as natron, or *net-jeryt*, that would dry out the flesh for forty days and harden the body for its eternal journey, so it took him a few minutes to dust himself off and follow the other workers outside.

Once Itennu's eyes adjusted to the bright daylight, he saw that a royal funeral barge was moored to the landing at the end of the narrow canal leading from the river to the House of Beauty. The corpse washers and other workers, maybe fifty in all, were crowded around a corpse on a sled elaborately decorated with gold and blue lotus flower patterns. The body itself, under layers of linen, was piled high with colorful and fragrant flowers under a white canopy that kept it in shade. The workers didn't know the identity of the sled's occupant, but they were busy taking bets as to who it might be before Bai announced the truth.

The skeletal Bai danced from one foot to the other in anxious negotiation with one of the older priests who had accompanied the corpse. As the negotiation drew to a close, the family members who had walked beside the corpse on its short trip from the boat landing to the Place of Purification turned and walked back toward the boat. In that instant, Itennu saw a possible means of escape from his prison. Queen Isis, her head bowed in sadness with the traditional dirt in her hair and torn clothing, walked under a sun canopy among several wailing harem women trailed by a handful of priests, their bald heads shiny with sweat in the hot afternoon sunlight. If Itennu could reach her, or even get close enough to call out and get her attention, she might take pity on his situation and free him from his bondage. All he had to do was get clear of the dozens of workers who would move to prevent his leaving as soon as they realized what he was trying to do.

He had to move before it was too late. He quickly determined a path that would take him around the crowd and out onto the stone dock that ran alongside the ceremonial river canal. His eyes were still trying to adjust to the unaccustomed glare of the bright sunlight, but he couldn't wait any longer, so he squinted and began to run.

As soon as he was around the mob, his feet hit the sturdy flat stone of the dock and he began to pick up speed. Breathing hard, he felt exhilarated by the chance of gaining his freedom again.

When his face hit the stone dock and the wind was knocked out of him, it took a moment for him to realize that someone had tackled him from behind. Groaning, he rolled over and saw the gap-toothed smile of Bai, the dancing skeleton, who quickly got up and began kicking him.

"Thought you could get away? You didn't want to leave all of your friends behind, did you?" With every question, Bai kicked him again. "After all we've done for you? After all the wonderful things we've taught you how to do? After we've revealed the mysteries of death and the meaning of life?"

Trying to protect the more fragile portions of his anatomy, Itennu rolled over and covered his head, noting as he did so that Queen Isis and her escort were back on the funeral barge.

The beating stopped as he heard the familiar voice of his mentor, Ay, yelling at Bai. "Enough! He's not going anywhere now!"

"The boy must learn," Bai hissed. "Nobody leaves here alive."

Itennu cautiously rolled on his side and looked back. Ay held the obsidian blade known as the Ethiopian Stone that was normally used by First Prophet Setau, the *Hery Sesheta*, to slice open the side of a corpse with the assistance of the Seal Bearer of Osiris. Ay had been waiting for the senior sem-priests to perform the ritual on a new body when the royal barge had arrived, interrupting everything.

"Bai, if you wish to make it back inside the House of Beauty alive, you'll leave the boy alone. I'll bring him in myself."

"You hold a blade on me? Your old friend? This is what it's come to after all these years?"

"You're nobody's friend, Bai." Ay might be short, fat, and old, but he certainly looked fierce with a weapon in his hand.

Bai slapped his chest. "Your words strike my heart."

Ay pointed the knife at Bai's chest. "My words or my blade. It's your choice."

Bai glared at Itennu before he walked away. "This isn't over, boy. Your dog won't always be around to protect you."

#

Having spent two nights in a jail pit near the temple of Ptah, Lord of Truth, Neferabu was happy to be out in the open air again, even if it meant that the day of his trial by the great court had arrived. Bandages of rough linen had been wrapped around his thigh and his torso to stop the bleeding after the Medjay arrows were plucked from his skin, but the pain of his injuries made his movements slow. He was alert, however, after spending most of a day unconscious following the rough removal of the arrows. He knew it was probably a good thing that he'd been unconscious for so long on the first day, as it had delayed the inevitable beatings of the following night. He felt alert after a second period of unconsciousness in the pit, but he was hungry. Prisoners generally weren't fed while they were being held for trial, especially when they weren't cooperative enough to confess to their crimes. He was pleased that Vizier To was in Thebes at the time of his capture, otherwise he might have died from starvation during a longer wait. The fact that he would be judged by the vizier also meant that his crime was serious enough to draw the great administrator's attention. The only higher judge was Pharaoh himself.

The trial would be held in the open air of the Karnak temple complex, allowing the curious to see the workings of truth and justice in the city's administration. Officials of the city sat in low chairs on a raised platform where they could see and hear everything clearly. The vizier would serve as both prosecutor and chief judge, but the other scribes and officials were allowed to observe, ask questions, and render opinions to the vizier before his final judgment. Some of them would have investigated

Neferabu's background and searched for the tomb that he and Khenti had robbed, although he doubted that they had found it since he and Khenti kept the entrance covered with rubble when they weren't inside.

The worst thing about the assembled nobles and scribes who would judge him was the fact that he knew most of them, and that most of them hated Neferabu. Although they had never seen him do so, his judges knew that Neferabu had slept with most of their wives. In his own defense, he had not sought out these relationships—the wealthy women of the city were some of his best clients. They came to him for paintings or finely sculpted statutes of themselves to decorate their tombs and their stately homes, knowing that the famous artist Neferabu was the best man for the job. He couldn't help it if they found him attractive. Despite all this, he doubted that their husbands would be predisposed to find him innocent of his crimes. He looked up at the sky, knowing that Amun-Re must hate him.

Sermont, the Medjay police captain, still holding Neferabu's tied wrists behind his back, suddenly pushed him down flat on his face, then placed his foot on Neferabu's back to keep him there. The warm sand felt good against Neferabu's skin. The murmur of the crowd increased when he heard rapid footsteps approaching.

Vizier To was about thirty years old, a young age for his great office, second only to Pharaoh in authority over the administration of the Two Lands; occasionally consulting with Bakenkhons, high priest of the Temple of Amun-Re, in matters of religious authority. He was a tall man who never smiled, most often displaying an expression of calm confidence that gave him a commanding presence. On this unusually hot morning, his bald head glistened as he strode toward the court after purifying himself in the sacred lake, his pleated white robes almost blinding white in the rays of the golden sun-boat just now rising above the eastern horizon. At the vizier's approach, the temple scribe Mai stood to announce him.

"Behold! The great Vizier To, Chief of the Six Courts of Justice, who judges the people and the inhabitants of the Two Lands, who hears causes, to whom the great come bowing down, and the whole land, prone upon the belly, waits to hear the words of his mouth, the words of judgment! In the name of the good god, his majesty Pharaoh Setnakhte, King of Upper and Lower Egypt, Chosen by Re, Beloved of Amun—life, prosperity, and health— in year four of his reign, the second month of Akhet, day 25! On this day in the great court of the city of Thebes, beside the two stelae of Ramesses the Great, in the forecourt of Amun-Re, by the great gate called Praise!"

Vizier To sat in the tallest chair, slightly ahead of his advisors, and placed his gold scepter of office across his chest. The chair, and his white-sandaled feet, were cushioned by pillows. A leather-wrapped scroll, the Book of Records, lay open on his lap. The crowd waited in silence as he nodded at Mai.

Mai held an arm out toward the officials on the platform. "Behold! Here, under the eye of the good god, his majesty Pharaoh Setnakhte—life, prosperity, and health—and of the great god, Amun-Re, in the presence of Maat, sits the great court of justice of this day, and the nobles and people who observe the great criminal Neferabu, and hear the words of his mouth. Behold the governor and vizier of Upper Egypt, the great To; the mayor of Thebes, Paweraa; the assistant to the high priest of the Temple of Amun-Re, Merubaste; the royal butler and scribe of Pharaoh's treasury, Pabasa; who sit in judgment on this day."

When Mai finished, Sermont lifted his foot from Neferabu's back and allowed him to rise to a kneeling position. Neferabu had sand in his mouth, but he was afraid to spit it out for fear of offending the vizier when he began to speak.

"Behold the great criminal, Neferabu, worker in the village of the Great Place! Having been examined severely in our presence, he has not confessed to the great crime of stealing from the tombs of those who dwell in eternity. He took an oath of Pharaoh—life, prosperity, and health—that he should be mutilated by cutting off his nose and his ears if he lied, saying he did not injure the tombs of the valley or steal from the nobles in their place!"

Neferabu suspected that Sermont would be more than happy to cut off his captive's nose and ears, no matter what the vizier decided. Sermont was also ready to beat him with the long wood staff he used like a walking stick, as he had already demonstrated more than once. No matter what happened, however, Neferabu would keep silent, confessing nothing, and hope that the great god Ptah did not force him to speak the truth from his own mouth, otherwise he might be executed before the day was over. Withholding the truth was also a crime against Maat that he would have to deal with when the time came for his judgment after death, but right now he just wanted to keep all of his face parts intact, along with his life.

Vizier To touched the golden figure of the winged goddess Maat that hung around his neck, and then looked directly at

Neferabu. "The great criminal, Neferabu, will now take a second oath before this tribunal, and before the gods, as he has been instructed."

Neferabu cleared his throat, wondering if he should bother to speak, then realizing that the less he cooperated, the more likely they were to kill him. "I will speak truthfully. I will not speak falsehood. Should witnesses be brought up against me that any property belonging to the tombs of the Great Place has been removed by me, I will be struck with one hundred blows, then my nose and ears will be cut off. Behold, this is the truth I say from my mouth on this day."

The crowd of onlookers parted to allow the passage of six burly priests carrying the statue of Ptah, Lord of Truth, within his golden shrine. Vizier To beckoned, and Merubaste stood up to approach the shrine of the god as it stopped beside the kneeling Neferabu, who was forced down on his face again by Sermont. Neferabu sighed, then angled his head so that he could watch the show.

Merubaste held two alternative statements written on papyrus, one in each hand held out wide from his body toward the golden shrine. Still holding them at arm's length, he tipped the papyrus in his left hand so that he could read from it. "O Ptah, Lord of Truth, my good lord; it is said that there is *no* crime against you by Neferabu, or matters that should be investigated in his case."

Neferabu liked the sound of that, but he knew there was another option. Merubaste tipped the papyrus in his right hand so that he could read from it. "O Ptah, Lord of Truth, my good lord; it is said that there *is* a great crime against you by Neferabu, and matters that should be investigated in his case."

Neferabu swallowed and watched the six priests holding the heavy shrine of the oracle on their shoulders. The shrine immediately tipped toward Merubaste's right hand. The god had spoken through them.

"The choice has been made," Merubaste said. "The great criminal Neferabu will be tried."

Neferabu wondered if he could just bury his head in the sand like an ostrich. The oracle, in the image of Ptah, might have just sentenced him to death.

#

Khenti had spent most of the night praying to various gods in his own house and in the small shrines in niches placed around the village of the workers. Only moonlight had illuminated his path through the narrow village streets, as he didn't want anyone to wake up and see his activity in the middle of the night. After hiding in their secret storage place by the river for a day, Ruta had returned to the village to tell Khenti of Neferabu's arrest. Remarkably, the artist who only thought of himself most of the time had drawn the Medjay away from the boy, allowing Ruta to escape.

Khenti spent many hours trying to figure out a way to help Neferabu without getting himself arrested, and how he and Ruta could leave the Great Place without attracting attention in a village where everyone knew everyone else's business. He finally decided that the Greek trading ships that smuggled tomb objects on the river might offer him a way out if he could board one without being seen. He certainly had enough money to buy passage somewhere safely away from Egypt, buy a trading ship or two, and become a merchant prince. He would offer Ruta the opportunity to go with him, otherwise the boy would likely suffer the same fate as Neferabu if he remained in the village.

When he pondered his options, Khenti realized that he knew one powerful official who wouldn't betray him and could offer help for Neferabu. While he worked at his normal job during the day, he had sent Ruta to deliver a message to Mayor Paweraa. Ruta's memory was good, so Khenti trusted him to remember his exact words. He would also send a gift of a gold *ushabti* figure to Paweraa, hinting that there would be more if the mayor could get Neferabu released from custody, or at least get his sentence reduced if he were already scheduled to appear in court. In the meantime, he had to hope that the normal process of interrogation by the Medjay had not prompted Neferabu to reveal Khenti's identity. He wouldn't blame Neferabu for exposing Khenti under torture, but he had to be ready to run if the Medjay came for him in the Great Place. Just in case, he kept a traveling bundle by the door that looked like the usual beer and lunch supplies he carried to work at the tombs each day. In this case, however, the beer jug was filled with gold and silver, and instead of food, the bundle carried the things he'd need for a long journey.

Khenti had also given Ruta a second task while he was in the city of Thebes. As one of the boys responsible for getting supplies to the village, Ruta could acquire large quantities of food without raising suspicion. The royal granaries normally made their grain wage deliveries to the village twice a month, but it was common for the privileged workers to order additional food from the markets in Thebes. So that Khenti wouldn't draw attention to himself, Ruta would buy a large quantity of grain and oils for delivery to the village, where Khenti would make arrangements to temporarily store the entire load until someone quietly delivered the supplies in small shipments to his own house, where his mother and sisters would remain after Khenti was gone. Khenti was the head of the household after his father had died, so if he left without providing for his mother's welfare, she and his sisters might be forced out of their home. His sisters could easily find work or marry an understanding husband, but his mother was too old to have those options. If she had no one to take care of her, and no means of support, she would probably have to leave the village she had known as her home for her entire life.

The one drawback to his plan was Neferabu. If Paweraa managed to get Neferabu released, it would probably occur after Khenti was gone. If he waited for Neferabu's return, he risked capture himself, along with Ruta. He saw no easy way in which Neferabu could leave with him on a trading ship, but Khenti would wait for him as long as he could. In the meantime, he would attend to his daily work as he always did, asking for help from the gods and hoping for the best.

#

Neferabu stared miserably at the gold heart scarab and staff of office that the Medjay had found him holding when he was captured. Khenti had apparently managed to hide everything else, most likely in their secret storage place by the river. The only good to come of all this was that Ruta had not been captured by the Medjay, allowing him to grow up and lead a normal life if he managed to keep his share of the wealth a secret from his family and friends in the village. Lying didn't come naturally to the boy, so he hoped that Ruta would learn this necessary skill as quickly as possible. Of course, if he considered his own situation objectively, he wasn't good at lying, either.

Ptah—Lord of Truth, chief god of craftsmen, and architect of the natural order of Maat in the Two Lands—was not pleased with Neferabu's performance in court. True, Neferabu had not made offerings to Ptah or the goddess Maat in many years, which might have helped him out now that he really needed it, because the gods remember such things, but it was too late to make amends. Once Ptah had determined that the court should rule on the case of Neferabu, he could only watch as the powerful men he'd offended sat in judgment over him, planning their revenge.

Kneeling in the sand before the vizier on his platform, Neferabu's heart skipped a beat when he saw Ruta in the crowd of onlookers. He was pretty sure that the boy had only recently appeared, but he was shocked to see that he was there in the first place because it was too dangerous. When Ruta saw Neferabu looking his way, he winked, nodded, and stepped back into the crowd, leaving him to wonder what the signal meant.

Neferabu had stopped listening to the vizier and his cronies of the court some time ago, assuming that the verdict was a foregone conclusion. The great Ptah hated him, the goddess of truth was ignoring him, and that was all he needed to know to foresee his own future. Now that Ruta had caught his interest, he studied the men of the court, who seemed to be haggling over the appropriate punishment for Neferabu's great crime against Pharaoh, the gods—and from the look of things—everyone seated on the platform.

Vizier To finally held up his hand. Merubaste, the fat priest of Amun-Re, nodded at his pals, lifted his bulk from the chair in an awkward motion, and waddled over to whisper in the vizier's ear. The vizier looked up at the sky, perhaps listening to the verdict of the gods, or feeling the breath of Horus upon his neck, then stood and spread his arms.

"Behold! We now have evidence that the great criminal Neferabu was aided in his crimes by one other man who will soon be punished, as all tomb robbers are punished who seek to defy Maat and the will of the gods!"

Neferabu sagged on his heels. Somehow, someone had managed to identify Khenti as his accomplice, and Khenti would probably assume that the informant was Neferabu. For a moment, he thought about Ruta standing in the crowd. Ruta was the only other person who knew. He shook his head in confusion, certain that Ruta would never have identified Khenti unless torture was involved, and that clearly hadn't happened. Who could have done it?

Once again, Neferabu was pushed flat on his face, getting sand in his eyes but managing to keep it out of his mouth this time. The weight of Sermont's enormous foot pressed down against his spine in case Neferabu tried to make a run for it while the verdict was being delivered—a wise move, since that was exactly what Neferabu was thinking of doing.

Neferabu blinked to clear his vision. The vizier frowned at him.

"Behold! The crimes of the great criminal Neferabu have

been examined and judged here in this place on this day. He is guilty of his crimes, so his punishment will cleave to him. His nose and his ears shall be removed from his head that the people may know of his great crimes, and he shall be transported to the mines of Timna, there to labor for the rest of his life. This is the punishment that shall be brought upon the great criminal Neferabu."

Neferabu closed his eyes. He wasn't going to die, but it was hard to get excited about that. He knew he would soon wish that he were dead.

#

"Hapu, my good friend, the omens are not good for you this day."

Mayor Paweraa stood beside the Temple of Ptah and shook his head as he looked down past his white sandals. A few feet below the grate, the haggard face of Hapu looked up at him from the pit. His face streaked with dirt, Hapu looked as if it had been a long time since he'd slept.

"Fortunately, I don't believe in omens," Hapu said, crossing his arms.

Paweraa smiled and pulled a loaf of bread out of a cloth bag hanging from his waist. The right bait was needed to bring Hapu to his senses. "You must be hungry. You've been in that hole for days."

"I haven't worked up much of an appetite down here. The only exercise I've had is brushing the dust off my head after people walk by."

Paweraa knelt down on the grate, ignoring the foul smell

from below, and snapped the bread loaf in half. "Then you wouldn't want this?"

Hapu eyed the bread. "I didn't say that."

"Would you confess to your great crimes if I gave you this bread?"

"I've committed no crimes, great or otherwise."

"An unfortunate attitude," Paweraa said, biting off a chunk of the bread. It was yesterday's bread, and it tasted stale, but he pretended to enjoy it. "At his trial in the place of examination this morning, the tomb painter also said that he had committed no crimes. However, the great Ptah exposed his lies, just as he will expose yours."

Hapu didn't seem impressed. Paweraa wondered if hunger and too much time in the dark hole had addled Hapu's wits.

"I will place my trust in the gods," Hapu said, briefly raising his arms toward the blue sky. "Maat will protect me. Ptah will protect me. On the day of examination, they will clear my name, for I have done nothing wrong."

"So you say, yet I have a witness. The tomb painter identified you as his accomplice when he was robbing the tombs."

"What? Who is this tomb painter?"

"Neferabu."

Hapu shook his head. "I know of no man with that name." Then he frowned.

Paweraa paused a moment, waiting to see if Hapu would take the bait. "He seems to know you quite well. Are you sure you've never heard of him?"

"There was a young man at the festival in Pi-Ramesses—"

"So you admit that you know him?"

"No, I—"

Paweraa stood and threw the bread down on the grate. "Enough of your lies! Must I have Sermont's men beat the confession out of you?"

"There has been a mistake," Hapu said in a calm voice. "I should not be here."

"Your mistake was greed. You've done so well for yourself, why did you also need trinkets from the tombs? How much wealth does one man need?"

"The great Ptah knows that I'm telling the truth," Hapu said, "and I shall prove it at the place of examination."

"Have it your way," Paweraa said, turning to walk away, impressed with his own performance. "I've done what I can for you. Neferabu has been sentenced, so perhaps you'll join him soon. Your fate is in the hands of the gods."

#

A young man in an elaborate black wig and pleated robes watched Paweraa stomp away from the pit where Hapu was trapped. When the mayor was a safe distance away, the young man staggered forward, apparently having imbibed too much beer, his arms loaded with many supplies from the local marketplace. When he reached the grate, he stumbled and fell with a loud grunt, dropping the bread, dates, and other foods. Other pedestrians on the crowded street just rolled their eyes and walked around him, grumbling about the decay of public decency and drunks wandering around among the sacred temples of Thebes, surely horrifying the gods.

The young man groaned and rolled on his side, looking down

at Hapu, who was busy collecting the numerous small foods that had dropped through the holes in the grate.

"Are you okay?" Ray asked.

"Much better now," Hapu said. "Your daily deliveries are what keep me going. You're a fine and faithful son. Now, get out of here before Paweraa comes back or someone sees what you're doing."

"They haven't caught on so far."

"All it takes is for the mayor, or Sermont, or one of his thugs to notice you just once. Your disguise won't help if they get a close look at you."

"Did the mayor have any good news?"

Hapu snorted, biting into a chunk of bread. "He says he has a witness to my crimes."

"That's impossible!"

"Of course it is, but witnesses can be bought or otherwise convinced to lie in the place of examination. Just the threat of torture turns most men into spineless worms. They'll say anything to save themselves."

"Who is this witness?"

"Neferabu the artist. The one we met in Pi-Ramesses."

Ray gasped. "Paweraa is lying. Neferabu is a tomb painter from a respected family. He'd never do such a thing."

Hapu shrugged. "We really know nothing about him. One confession is as good as another as far as Paweraa and the other judges are concerned."

Ray rose to his knees. "I'll go and speak with him myself. He must have made a mistake."

"It's too late. Neferabu has been examined and sentenced.

To visit him now would only throw suspicion on yourself, and probably get you captured."

"But—"

"Do not concern yourself, my son." Hapu raised his arms to the sky. "I've led a good life so far, and I expect it to continue. The gods will protect me."

"They better do so soon before it's too late."

Hapu hesitated, then frowned. "I want to remind you of something. Your duty is to protect Bull, no matter what happens. You are also very important, but in a different way, and we will need to discuss this matter in more detail after I'm free of this prison. Now that you're old enough, you need to understand your responsibilities as an adult and the sacrifices you may have to make for the good of Egypt. We can't discuss this now, but I wanted to remind you of your duty—keep Bull safe, but protect yourself as well. Stay hidden until you can return to the golden house and meet with the living god Ramesses or his father, because they are the only ones who have the knowledge to help you. Do you understand?"

"We'll get you out, father."

"Do you understand?" he yelled.

"Yes, father." Startled, Ray couldn't remember the last time he'd seen his father speak to him in anger.

Hapu closed his eyes and took a calming breath. "Good. That's good. I'm sorry I yelled at you. I just can't be certain we'll have another chance to talk."

"Khamenwati has a plan to rescue you if all else fails, but is there anything else you wish me to do, father?"

Hapu lowered his arms and thought about it a moment.

"Perhaps you and Khamenwati could make some offerings for me—to Ptah, Maat, Thoth, and Amun-Re—just in case the gods have been too busy to notice me."

#

Now that Khait had spent a week with Shepsit learning to be a priestess of Hathor, her lessons got harder. The walled administrative and residential complex below Hatshepsut's mortuary temple was relatively simple in design compared to the administrative centers for some of the others on the west bank, such as the Temple of Amun-Re where a visitor could get lost for a day. However, the loving and motherly nature of Hathor was reflected in her buildings, creating an intimate and comfortable environment in which new priestesses could learn and established priestesses could manage the many daily tasks required to run a major temple and serve the goddess.

Hathor herself had many roles to play. In Thebes, Hathor helped to protect the necropolis as Goddess of the Western Mountain, but she also personified love, beauty, sexuality, childbirth, and rebirth. In the Eastern Desert, she was worshipped as the goddess of mountains and minerals at Egypt's mines. As a priestess of Hathor, Khait was most focused on Hathor's aspect as the queen of happiness and goddess of music, dance, and intoxication. Over the first week of her training, four full nights were spent increasing her stamina and ability to cross the threshold that separated the world of mortals from the sphere of the gods. Learning the secret of this mystery involved drinking the strong ritual wine, mixed with blossoms of the blue lotus, and dancing throughout the night with other priestesses as fires burned sweet-smelling myrrh incense around the perimeter of the temple courtyard. The dances varied, but they were all ener-getic, and often required rapid swinging movements of the head that made Khait too dizzy to stand until she got used to the feeling. At times, the weights tied to the ends of her narrow hair braids brushed the ground when she bent low. The wine didn't help with her balance, but she understood how the ritual was enhanced by it. After they were warmed up from the first dance and Khait really felt the effects of the wine, Shepsit made them all bow and raise their outstretched arms toward the sky as she began one of the chants that Khait had started to learn:

#

Come, O Golden Goddess,
the singers chant.
For it is nourishment for the heart to dance the iba,
to shine over the feast at the hour of retiring,
and to enjoy ha-dance at night.
Come! The procession takes place at the site of drunkenness,
the area where one wanders in the marshes.
Its routine is set, the rules are firm,
nothing is left to be desired.
The royal children satisfy You with what You love,
and the officials give offerings to You.
The lector priest exalts You singing a hymn,
and the wise men read the rituals.
The priest honors You with his basket,
and the drummers take their tambourines.
Ladies rejoice in Your honor with garlands,
and girls do the same with wreaths.
Drunkards play tambourines for You in the cool night,

and those they wake up bless You.
The Bedouin dance for You in their garments,
and Asiatics dance with their sticks.
The griffins wrap their wings around You,
the hares stand on their hind legs for You.
The hippopotami adore with wide open mouths,
and their legs salute Your face.

#

Khait wore only a short sash tied around her waist and a heavy *menit*-necklace with beads that rattled. Each dancer carried a sistrum that they would shake in time with the music played by blind harpists and tambourine players they only saw as dim shapes beyond the flaming braziers. In her other hand, Khait gripped a copper mirror with a handle shaped like the head of Hathor with her beautiful face, long hair, and cow ears. Each dancer's *ka*, or soul, was reflected in her mirror, and Khait was often startled to see how her reflection would change during mirror dances as the night wore on. The rhythm of this exhausting ritual every other night would often lead to mystical communion with Hathor, evoking visions of the past or future, life among the gods, or simply of distant friends or relatives. Khait sometimes saw herself talking with animals, plants, or stones, and her visions often filled her with feelings of awe, joy, or love. When clouds of incense drifted across the courtyard, Khait sometimes felt as if she were flying or drifting on the breeze with a joyful lightness of being. It was during one of these drifting visions that she first met Hathor.

The goddess was in her human form wearing her crown of cow horns encircling the sun disk. Her large breasts were proudly exposed above her high-waisted red sheath dress. Khait did her best to prostrate herself at the feet of Hathor, but the goddess simply smiled and gestured for Khait to face her. The darkness swirled around the two of them and nothing else seemed to exist. No words were exchanged, but Khait felt excited and loved. Then Hathor's face gradually shifted to a woman's face that looked very familiar. After a few moments, Khait realized the face belonged to an older version of herself— her mother, Afrikaisi, who had died when Khait was eight years old. Filled with sadness, Khait felt tears running down her face, and a deep sense of loss, but this quickly changed to a sense of euphoria when Afrikaisi smiled at her and she realized she had found a way to commune with her mother in the afterlife. When her mother nodded and turned to walk away, she faded into the darkness and Khait found herself lying exhausted on the floor of the courtyard. Many hands lifted her and she fell asleep, waking several hours later on her sleeping pallet in the tiny cell she called her bedroom.

Khait was ravenous, but when she rolled onto her side she saw that a servant had kindly left a tray of figs, dates, bread, and milk on the small table by her bedside. The priestesses were not allowed to eat the day before a dance ritual would be performed, but they could eat and sleep as much as they wanted on the days of rest, as long as they performed a their chores in the afternoons. Many of the priestesses were still serving the goddess at the Opet Festival, so Khait's chores involved cleaning the Hathor shrine inside Hatshepsut's mortuary temple and removing any offerings brought by visitors so that the food could be distributed among the priestesses before it went bad. Offerings of gold, silver, or precious stones were to be deposited in the temple treasury, but Khait had seen none of those so far, probably because Hathor was still at the Opet Festival. With so few visitors, there wasn't any need for a senior priestess to sit hidden within the stairwell behind the shrine where she could answer visitors' questions with the voice of Hathor. While Khait cleaned the shrine, she thought back on the vision of her mother and euphoria filled her once more, making her skin tingle as she realized that her initiation into the mysteries of Hathor had now given her a new confidence and the security of knowing for certain that her life would continue after death in the Field of Reeds.

Shepsit had warned her not to discuss her visions with anyone else, even though she was bursting to share her experience with the other priestesses. However, she also knew they were keeping their distance from her as a means to help with her initiation. She would see other dancers at the night rituals, but they were in their own worlds. Khait had the sense that she would remain at the outer edges of this community until she had completed her learning and understood enough of the mysteries, Shepsit had said it took some women many months of service before they experienced clear visions and the learning that came with them, but there would come a time when a final decision would be made. At that time, Khait would either be sent away forever, or she would be allowed to become a full priestess. Having made good progress with her dancing, she felt the support of Hathor and strongly believed she was doing the right thing. Her fate was to join the temple. The only thing that worried her now was what life would be like when she had to go back out into the real world and return to her service in the golden house.

Two nights later and many hours into the ritual, Khait started her second mirror dance. Shepsit had informed her beforehand that she was gradually increasing the strength of the lotus blossom added to the ritual wine as Khait adapted to its effects and was better able to continue her dance throughout the night. Shepsit also directed her to remain open to any experiences Hathor wished to provide, but that she could also seek answers to questions through focus during the dance. Although it was up to Hathor whether or not to bestow knowledge by answering their questions, Shepsit always consulted the goddess to help others or before she made important life decisions, and the mirror helped to focus her intent.

Khait stared into the mirror as she spun. Clouds of incense drifted across the courtyard and the rhythm of several rattling sistra combined with the strumming of lutes and harps to create a fluid blanket of sound around her sweating body. After the first couple of hours, her hunger pangs passed and the drugged wine smoothed her movements and her thoughts. Now, two hours before dawn, with the moonless night as dark as it could be, she felt another presence nearby. The mirror looked darker now, flashing when it reflected the fires burning in their braziers as she kept spinning, but her own reflected face moved into the background to be joined by another.

It was Ray.

Ray stood on broad watersteps washed by the sparkling waters of the Nile. He looked prosperous and happy. He also looked taller and much more muscular than she remembered. Khait smelled water, wet mud, papyrus reeds, and fish. Beside Ray, Prince Ramesses IV dangled his legs in the gurgling water.

After handing his black wig to a white-robed priest, Ray removed a beautiful kilt and his jewelry, then dove into the river with the prince. Khait knew she was there with them, but when she raised her hand to her face it looked older.

Startled and shaky, nearly dropping her mirror, Khait sat down hard on the flat stone of the courtyard. She saw only her face in the mirror now, but the faint smell of the Great River still lingered in her nostrils.

Shepsit loomed over her. "Are you all right?"

Khait nodded, unable to speak.

"You had a vision. Something new and powerful."

Khait nodded again.

"Don't think about it too much. Let it rest in your heart. The goddess will help you understand what you have seen, but it may take some time."

"Yes," she croaked.

Shepsit smiled and held out her hand. "You have done well, my child. Hathor favors you with knowledge. It has been some time since any of our initiates advanced so quickly." She helped Khait get to her feet and gave her a hug. "You may rest now. There is more to learn."

Three

1184 BCE—City of Abydos

Year 4 of His Majesty, King of Upper and Lower Egypt, Chosen by Re, Beloved of Amun, Pharaoh Setnakhte, Second Month of Akhet (Season of Inundation), Day 26

#

After almost two weeks of driving the chariot across the desert, following the fastest trade routes that connected with the major towns along the Nile, a great sense of relief washed over Didu and Nebamun when they saw the sacred city of Abydos—greatest of all the cemeteries and home to Osiris, god of the underworld. Having reached Abydos, they knew they were within a day of reaching Thebes, their ultimate objective, where they were most likely to find the kidnappers of the crown prince, Ramesses IV.

Abydos was unusually clean when compared to most of the cities along the river, its white limestone and whitewashed mud-brick buildings always gleaming in the sun. Most of the residents worked for the Temple of Osiris, spending much of their time maintaining the temple, the sacred city, and the massive necropolis that had been occupied since the time of the earliest pharaohs. Although Nebamun had never visited Abydos, Didu remembered attending festivals there as a child, uncomfortably aware that millions of the dead also made an annual pilgrimage from their tombs to worship Osiris in his home. This was a temple of great power, for this was where the head of Osiris, Lord of the Dead, was buried.

When they arrived inside the city, Didu noticed that there were only a few people moving about in the streets. Although it was still early in the morning, the increasing heat of the day would normally prompt the citizens to get their outdoor activities done before the golden boat of the sun was high overhead.

"I need beer," Nebamun said, slapping Didu on the shoulder as they stepped down from the chariot. "I've got enough sand in my throat to gag a hippo."

Didu gestured at the entrance to a neighborhood beer hall as he walked around the chariot to tie down the horses. "Maybe we should have warned them that you were coming. We don't want to drink their entire supply."

"You think they've heard about me?"

"I wouldn't be surprised. You know how tongues wag in the army. Even the residents of Abydos, dead or alive, must have heard the stories."

Nebamun seemed pleased with himself. "Excellent point."

When Didu and Nebamun ducked through the low doorway, they discovered a beer hall that was oddly silent, just like the rest of the city. No people or animals were in sight.

"Slow day," Nebamun said. "More for us to drink."

"You don't suppose there's a festival today, do you? It was

quiet outside, too." There were so many festivals in so many cities, it was hard to keep track unless you were a priest or one of the locals who always attended. The annual Nile flood was a popular time of year for pilgrimages to the cities. With their fields flooded, the farmers were able to take a break and attend the festivals.

"Festival or not, I'm still thirsty," Nebamun said, striding toward the back of the dark hall.

A small boy, maybe eight years old, stepped out through a doorway in the back. "We're closed."

Nebamun stopped in his tracks. "Why?"

The boy cocked his head. "Don't you know? It's the Going Forth of Osiris."

Nebamun glanced at Didu, who shrugged.

"What kind of a celebration will it be without beer? That's barbaric."

The boy laughed. "You don't know anything. There's plenty of beer at the temple, and it's free. That's why we're closed."

Nebamun smiled and patted the boy's head. "You're a good lad. May the gods watch over you."

"If you hurry, there's still time to see the Great Procession."

Nebamun looked at Didu, who nodded. "Procession first, beer later. That's how it works."

"Then I'd love to see the procession," Nebamun said, heading for the door.

#

The Great Procession was part of the Great Going Forth, in which the body of the god Osiris was carried from the temple in the funeral boat—the *Neshmet* barge. If they had arrived one day earlier, Didu knew they could have seen the reenactment of the murder of Osiris by the evil god Set. Two women, representing the goddesses Isis and Nephthys, would anxiously search the city and the river until they found the scattered body parts of Osiris. The body would then be taken to the temple and ritually mummified for the funeral procession on the second day.

When Didu and Nebamun arrived in the neighborhood of the Temple of Osiris, they found that the Neshmet barge had already passed through the streets on its way to the Sacred Lake of Abydos. Working their way through the crowd, they arrived in time to see the boat drift past on the lake, which symbolized the passage of Osiris from the sphere of the living to the land of the dead. During this passage, Osiris became the sovereign of the deceased, "the one who presides over the westerners." The people cheered during this entire ritual, knowing that Osiris would lie in his tomb for only a few days before he was resurrected as an immortal. The resurrection of Osiris, which also represented the triumph over death that most people expected for themselves, was the joyous occasion that would complete the festival at Abydos.

Didu and Nebamun worshipped in their own way, by returning to the Temple of Osiris to consume the first of the beer that the priests put out for the faithful. While Didu was respectful of Osiris, he had already done his duty to the god by attending the funeral procession, so he didn't see any need to stay around and think about his own death. Watching Nebamun drink his third jar of beer, he knew that this was a man who never worried about death at all—not out of sheer courage, but more because it just never occurred to him. There was something to be said for that way of life.

Sipping at his beer, Didu wondered how long they would have to wait before the priests put out the free food. He guessed that the priests would probably delay until evening. The food had to stretch for eight more days while the scattered body parts of Osiris were "found" by the goddesses and the priests had mummified and resurrected the god from the House of Gold, which they preferred to do in secret. After the priests raised the Djed Pillar—the backbone of Osiris—the final big feast would start, although Didu didn't plan to stay in Abydos to wait for it. He was already anxious to leave.

"What do you think of the beer?" Didu asked.

"Not very good," Nebamun said, picking up his fourth jar of beer and sniffing at it. "I don't like the kind with fruit in it."

"It's festival beer. At least it's filling. Maybe it's not supposed to taste as good as regular beer since we're supposed to be thinking about death."

"Maybe that's why it's free."

The wailing of women attracted their attention once more. The young women playing the parts of Isis and Nephthys drifted through the crowd with graceful, sweeping arcs of their bare arms as they wailed in unison. Their wispy gowns flowed behind them like water rippling in the wake of a boat. Wherever they went, the people bowed and allowed them to pass. Didu recognized one of them as a famous dancer he'd seen at many festivals. When he saw the second woman, he nearly choked on his beer when he realized how much she looked like the beautiful young princess Tentopet, daughter of the great Pharaoh Ramesses III.

Nebamun winked at him. "She's a nice one, eh?"

"Does she look familiar to you?"

"I wish she did," Nebamun said, wiping his mouth and leering at her.

"Are you sure, Neb? Did you look carefully?"

"I assure you that I did, my old friend. I have committed her to memory. Why so interested?"

Didu continued to watch the two women recede into the crowd, circling their way back toward the far end of the lake. They would meet the boat when the statue of Osiris was lifted onto the waiting funeral sled for its journey to the tomb.

Didu shook his head. "She looked familiar, but that would be impossible. The beer must be getting to me."

"You've only had two jars."

Didu put his empty jar down on the serving table. "We should be going. I'd like to reach Thebes by nightfall."

Nebamun grabbed three more jars of beer and held them in his arms. "I'm ready."

Didu glanced at the distant figures of the wailing women once more, wondering why the princess Tentopet would be in Abydos without any other women of the harem, then turned and led the way back to the chariot. He had his orders to hunt down the kidnappers, which took priority over anything else he might see along the way, so it was best not to improvise. Pharaoh had given him a mission that didn't allow failure. He was quite fond of his head and planned to keep it firmly attached to his body.

#

Still dressed in the pleated robe of fine linen and the long black wig of a noble, Ray stood in the middle of the crowd watching his father's trial at the place of examination. Ray knew that Vizier To, Merubaste, Mayor Paweraa, or one of the other officials on the dais might recognize him, disguised or not, so he remained in the shadow of a massive lotus pillar that held up the white limestone roof high overhead. Bull was safely hidden away for the morning among the student scribes in Khamenwati's class so that Ray wouldn't have to worry about him.

So far, the examination of Hapu wasn't going very well. To Ray's surprise, the oracle had indicated that the evidence against Hapu should be investigated. That made him worry more, as his father had been certain that the gods would support him. Of course, it was hard to be sure what the gods were thinking—Ptah might have wanted to make sure his father's name was cleared of any suspicion by considering all of the evidence.

There were three types of evidence that mattered in this particular case: physical evidence, such as that found at Hapu's home by Sermont; gossip, of which there was plenty when successful people were brought to the place of examination; and witnesses. Despite Hapu's innocence, a witness had come forth to identify Hapu as a conspirator in raiding the wealth of the tombs in the Great Place, and that testimony had been recorded and read to the assembled judges by Mai, the temple scribe. Since the story told by the witness had been "verified" with a thorough beating, his account held great weight with the vizier and his court. Hapu's strongest points were his reputation and his responsible high office in Pharaoh's service, but the physical evidence found at his home made it harder for the judges to believe in his innocence.

Finally, seeing the frustrated expression on the vizier's face, and the disinterested expressions of his other judges, Hapu's last resort was flattery. Vizier To's hereditary position, second only to Pharaoh in the administration of Upper Egypt, was difficult and complex, but it was also an unpopular position. A vizier had no friends and many enemies.

When Hapu was allowed to speak again, he cleared his throat. "Chief Steward, Vizier of Upper Egypt, my lord, you are the greatest of the great, you are the guide to all that which is not and that which is. When you embark upon the sea of truth, the winged goddess Maat fills your sails with justice and guides your path to wisdom. You are father to the orphan, husband to the widow, brother to the desolate, garment for the motherless. The great bow down before you and honor your name. They are but dust upon your feet. Let me place your name in this land higher than all good laws, for you guide without avarice, you are free of corruption, and you create truthfulness in upholding justice and the balance of Maat. Throw the evil to the ground and do justice, you praised one whom the praised ones praise and the gods look upon with favor. Behold, remove my oppressive burden, the weight of the lies cast upon me. Behold, I am in sorrow, for my life and service to the good god, our Pharaoh, are as nothing beneath your gaze. Consider all that I have done, and will do, for the Two Lands, and how your name will be praised for your mercy and wisdom when I am released without sentence. Free me, my lord, for you are the light that guides the people of this land through the darkness of deceit, and you are truth."

Vizier To gave Hapu a brief smile and fingered the winged gold figure of Maat that hung from his neck. Mai remained focused on his papyrus scroll, his brush flashing across its surface as he strove to keep his notes caught up with everything that Hapu had just said. Watching the show on the dais, the crowd of onlookers buzzed with murmurs regarding Hapu's guilt or innocence. Merubaste grunted and rose from his seat, leaning forward to whisper something in the vizier's ear while he gestured at Hapu. The vizier frowned and stood up, gesturing for Merubaste to return to his place.

Ray wrapped his fingers around the figurine of Thoth in his pocket, praying that the god would give Vizier To the wisdom to see through the lies and return his father to freedom. When Vizier To took the unprecedented step of descending from the dais to approach Hapu, Ray's heart jumped and he moved forward to be closer to his father, keeping his head low among the crowd to minimize the possibility of his discovery.

The vizier stopped in front of Hapu and spoke with a soft voice, making it hard for the crowd to hear what he said. Straining to make out the words, Ray continued to edge closer.

"Scribe Hapu, noble teacher to Pharaoh's golden house, I ask you to understand the problem presented before me. Witnesses have described your activities as a tomb robber and defiler of the Great Place, for which the punishment is quite severe. What these witnesses, and the advisors seated beside me, cannot fully understand is that there are ramifications to punishment of one such as yourself. I have not survived this long as Vizier of Upper Egypt without understanding the ties that bind the powerful together, and the political misfortunes that come with public displays of justice where there may be doubt as to the motives or guilt of the great criminal I am to judge. These are uncertain times, made more difficult for me with unrest in Lower

Egypt that appears to be tied to the vizier—my brother in the administration of the Two Lands. Pharaoh is watching both of us carefully, knowing that we two are the keys to the flight of the youngest hawk and the flow of the Nile, as nothing happens in this land without the knowledge of the viziers. If one of the viziers cannot be trusted, we are both in peril. My movements and decisions are watched closely by Pharaoh's spies, which brings me back to the dilemma of your appearance before this court. I am not convinced of your guilt, despite evidence and witnesses to the contrary. Successful men always have enemies waiting to bring them low. You also have a long record of public service to the good god and the Two Lands. Were you in my position, I'm sure you would understand the sympathy I feel for your current predicament, as I might just as easily be kneeling there before this dais in your place. On the other hand, if you are guilty of the crimes laid out before this court, and I let you go free, my own position will again be in peril. And so, I ask you now directly, here in this place of examination, under the watchful gaze of Ptah and Maat, whether you are guilty of these great crimes."

Hapu shook his head. "I am innocent, my lord. As innocent as the day I was born. I swear this to be true under the eyes of Ptah. If I speak falsely, I will accept the pain of mutilation for these great crimes, which I did not do."

Vizier To studied Hapu's face, then shook his head. "I want to believe you, but there is too much at stake here. The eyes of Pharaoh—life, prosperity, and health—are upon us. I must consult the oracle."

The vizier strode back to his place on the dais and spoke

with Merubaste, who signaled to a group of waiting priests. A moment later, the priests carried the statue of Ptah up to the kneeling Hapu, where it remained on their shoulders. Merubaste came forward with a piece of papyrus in each outstretched hand, through which the god could communicate his decision regarding Hapu's guilt or innocence.

"O Ptah, Lord of Truth, you have heard the words of the great criminal Hapu's mouth, and those of the witness to his great crime of defiling the tombs of the Great Place. We now ask you to show us your wisdom and manifest your wishes by inclining your head."

Ptah's statue, still resting on the shoulders of the tired priests, tipped toward Merubaste's right hand. Merubaste raised the chosen papyrus to his face so that he could read the verdict.

"The decision has been made," Merubaste said, frowning at Hapu. "The great lord Ptah, here on this day in the presence of the officials of the place of examination, has examined the crimes of the great criminal Hapu and found that he has committed them. The officials gathered here on this day will cause Hapu's punishment to cleave to him."

Merubaste turned and gave a slight bow to the vizier, seated once more on his chair, his staff held across his chest.

A brief look of pain clouded the vizier's face, but he cleared his throat, gazed straight into Hapu's eyes, and pronounced the sentence. "Behold! The crimes of the great criminal Hapu have been examined and judged here in this place on this day. He has committed these crimes, and they have taken hold of him, so his punishment will cleave to him. His nose and his ears shall be struck from his head so that the people may know of his great crimes, and he shall be transported to the royal mines of Timna, there to labor for the rest of his life. This is the punishment that shall be brought upon the great criminal Hapu."

Hapu's eyes closed and his body sagged. Sermont and one of his thugs lifted Hapu's limp form and led him away. Mayor Paweraa, seated in silence throughout most of Hapu's examination, rose from his chair with great dignity and approached the vizier, speaking in a soft voice.

Ray couldn't believe what he had just heard. Although Khamenwati had created a backup plan to get Hapu released in the event that he was found guilty, Ray had not believed that the great Ptah would abandon his faithful Hapu. Since Hapu's capture, Ray had reinforced Ptah's good sentiments toward his father with several sacrifices before Ptah's shrine as well as the other gods his father had specified. The gods had failed them, believing the lies about Hapu's participation in the tomb robberies. How was this possible?

Straining to hear the quiet words that Paweraa spoke to the vizier, Ray edged closer to the dais, stopping when the vizier glared at the mayor and shook his head.

"He has performed great service to the golden house of Pharaoh!"

Paweraa raised his hands in a conciliatory gesture. "I do agree. I merely suggest that the punishment you have prescribed, an exception for a man of high office, may establish an unfortunate precedent. We should consider the future."

Perhaps there was hope for his father. Ray wanted to hear more, but he saw Sermont coming his way and knew that he had to move before he was recognized. While the mayor and the vizier continued their discussion, Ray turned and walked away, knowing it was time to contact Khamenwati.

#

The massive black bird head loomed two feet taller than the startled humans in the street, although it rested atop a human-like figure draped in a robe of white ibis feathers. The bird's long, narrow beak, hooked at the end, looked sharp enough to tear the heart out of anyone who might interfere with its progress. Any observer knew immediately that this was the god of wisdom and writing, as well as spokesman for all of the gods—the great Lord Thoth.

The unblinking black eyes of the great man-bird stared straight ahead, defying anyone to stop him as he strode forward with only his white-sandaled feet sometimes visible beneath the feather cape, making it appear that he floated rather than walked. The gold collar on his chest reflected the late afternoon sunlight. The onlookers in his path knew enough to back away and bow, their arms outstretched in submission and respect. A train of almost one hundred student scribes, dressed in white robes, trailed behind the god with their writing tools while banging on hand drums and rattling sistra in rhythm with their steps. The senior teacher of the scribe school, Khamenwati, walked just ahead of his students and a few steps behind Thoth, his writing kit in one hand while he used his ibis-headed ivory cane with the other.

That morning, the great criminal Hapu had been found guilty of his crimes and received his sentence for punishment by Vizier To. The next morning, he was to receive his punishment. When the Medjay guard, standing in the shade of a doorway near

Hapu's jail pit, saw the god approach along the street and stop above Hapu's place of imprisonment, he knew better than to remain in the neighborhood and possibly incur the god's wrath, as Thoth could only have appeared in this place at this time for one reason.

Thoth stopped above Hapu's pit and the student scribes formed a great circle around him. The crowd of onlookers remained in place along the sides of the street, heads bowed with eyes raised to watch the spectacle. The running footsteps of the retreating Medjay guard, and the rhythmic rattle of the sistra carried by some of the students, were the only sounds that broke the silence.

Khamenwati raised his ivory cane high and spoke to the crowd as Thoth gazed into the distance. "The great god Thoth has come among us to protest a great crime of justice! He is here to visit his faithful scribe, Hapu, unjustly accused of robbing the tombs of the Great Place!"

As Khamenwati spoke, Thoth used his magic to shrink among the throng of scribes, his head slowly descending to human height and below, finally vanishing from the crowd's view.

Khamenwati kept his staff raised as he turned in a circle to look at the crowd. "The great god Amun-Re reminds us that even though we might not receive justice in this world, the innocent will still have the rewards of the afterworld. However, Amun-Re must sometimes work through the other gods to right the wrongs of the present day. Behold Lord Thoth, his messenger!"

Khamenwati closed his eyes to chant:

#

Amun-Re who first was king,
The god of earliest time,
The vizier of the poor.
He does not take bribes from the guilty,
He does not speak to the witness,
He does not look at him who promises,
Amun judges the land with his finger.
He speaks to the heart,
He judges the guilty,
He assigns him to the East,
The righteous to the West.

#

When Khamenwati finished his chant, the head of the Lord Thoth slowly rose above the surrounding students and on up to his full height once more, still gazing off into the future with his enigmatic bird expression.

Khamenwati opened his eyes. "The messenger of the gods has visited the scribe Hapu and verified his innocence! Thoth now demands that Hapu be released to return to his duties as teacher to the children in the golden house of Pharaoh! Those who defy him shall meet Thoth's judgment in the afterworld, where their hearts will be eaten by the goddess Ammut—Eater of Hearts—and they will face the true death!"

Thoth strode forward once more as Khamenwati and the student scribes resumed their positions trailing along behind him in the procession. Once again, the crowd parted to clear the god's path. A low murmur of worried voices indicated that the onlookers had understood the dire consequences of Thoth's threat. The vizier would have to release Hapu or face the worst punishment imaginable, along with any others who had unjustly accused Hapu.

Mayor Paweraa and Sermont arrived at the edge of the crowd after being summoned by the Medjay guard, who had refused to return with them to face Thoth. Having heard the last part of Khamenwati's speech, they were aware of Thoth's anger at Hapu's treatment. As Thoth and the procession started away, Paweraa spoke to Sermont, who then charged ahead.

Jogging over to the pit where Hapu had been imprisoned, Paweraa lifted the grate and looked into its shadows. "The pit is empty!"

The startled Khamenwati had no time to react as Sermont lunged and tackled the god. Thoth fell on his face and the clay bird head rolled away from the man's body, exposing Hapu, who struggled to get free of both Sermont and the feathered cloak that surrounded him. Khamenwati jumped on Sermont's back, but his light weight was easily cast aside. Four more Medjay policemen showed up to assist Sermont, punching and kicking Hapu to demonstrate why he shouldn't have tried to escape.

Ray then burst through the front rows of the student scribes. Before he could reach Hapu and Sermont, Bull grabbed Ray's arms and pulled him back. Khamenwati was lifted to his feet by two students. Coordinated as if they were a military unit, the scribes then formed a protective wall around Ray and their teacher, hustling them through the confused crowd to safety while the Medjay were still distracted.

#

Didu and Nebamun did not have a hard time finding the house of Hapu in Thebes. It seemed that everyone they spoke to had heard of Hapu and knew where he lived, which seemed odd since he normally spent so much of his time at the golden house of Pharaoh. On their arrival at Hapu's home, they found out why. Biti, the ancient servant, opened the red granite door and admitted them to a delightful courtyard with a formal garden of mature fruit trees arranged around a rectangular pond that reflected the moonlight. Biti had little understanding of why Hapu had been singled out by the Medjay for punishment, and he complained about the ridiculous trial he had witnessed earlier that day, but he mostly seemed worried about his future employment. From what Didu knew of Hapu's reputation, he thought it unlikely that the teacher of Pharaoh's children would bother with stolen tomb goods, but so much mystery surrounded Hapu's recent actions that it was hard to form an opinion. Perhaps Hapu had many secrets that only a skilled interrogator would be able to uncover. The Medjay had a long tradition of working for Pharaoh as border guards and city peacekeepers, but they had not been trained in Pharaoh's army, and Didu suspected that their skills were limited with regard to prisoner handling and interrogation.

An hour later, after a general search through Hapu's house and grounds that revealed no new clues as to where Hapu's two companions might have gone, they passed once more through the red granite door into the street. As they started away, Didu noticed a shadowy figure in a doorway that stepped out to follow them.

Nebamun nudged Didu with his elbow and spoke in a low voice. "You saw him?"

Didu nodded. "Could be someone out for a walk. Maybe he can't sleep."

They made a few turns down side streets. Their shadow varied his distance behind them, but continued to keep them in view. When they spotted a deep alcove in a dark alley, they ducked into it and crouched down to wait.

"Want me to take him?" Nebamun asked.

"Not yet. I want to see where he goes."

When the big man appeared in the street, they saw he was wearing the pleated white robes of a priest. Nebamun snorted and started to stand up, but Didu held him back and gestured for him to remain silent. The priest looked into the alley and they saw he had a beard. Although it didn't seem right, Didu figured the man might be from the rural temple of some minor god who required his priests to be bearded. The priest turned slowly in place, listening in different directions, then growled and stalked away.

Nebamun looked at Didu. "That was odd. Did you see his beard?"

"Let's follow him."

Ten minutes later, the priest walked into the bright glow of an open beer hall door. The beer hall was one of many known as the Eye of Horus, identified by the sparkling sign made of green malachite above the doorway that displayed the well-known symbol of the eye in the pyramid. A businessman from Memphis, known as Panahasi, had opened the first Eye of Horus about ten years earlier, and now one could find his beer halls on almost every street corner of every major city along the Nile. Panahasi brewed his own fresh beer, known as *Pharaoh's Favorite*, from a secret family recipe that started with beer bread crumbled over a sieve, sweetened with dates, washed with water, then left to ferment into a thick, sweet beer. Panahasi's breweries produced this beer in a central location in each city, then supplied the product to his beer halls. He also supplied his beer to temples during religious festivals where local officials and the nobility preferred a better beer than would be provided to the masses. Opinions varied about Pharaoh's Favorite, and the less expensive Eye of Horus beers, but it had established its own cult of devoted followers and Panahasi had become a wealthy man. Independent beer hall owners who resisted the opening of a new Eye of Horus in their neighborhoods were likely to either be put out of business through lack of customers or acquired and turned into an Eye of Horus themselves. Panahasi had powerful friends who were loyal to his beer, he paid his taxes, and he never visibly harmed anyone, so he was allowed to run his business without official interference.

Didu thought all of the Eye of Horus beers were too expensive, and didn't really taste any different from regular beer, but as soon as Nebamun saw the priest go into the beer hall, he was through the door an instant later. Before he followed, Didu took the time to look through one of the beer hall windows. The bearded priest sat at a table with three others dressed in similar attire, who had all greeted the new arrival with angry shouts. Didu couldn't hear what they were saying over the noise of the other patrons in the beer hall, but Nebamun was seated at a table beside the priests where he quickly drained a beer jar, ignoring the drinking bowl on his table. After a moment, Neb said something to the priests and one of them responded with an angry growl. Worried that his friend might do something stupid, Didu rushed inside.

In the time it took for Didu to enter the beer hall and navigate past the fancy carved furniture to Nebamun's table, two more beer jars had appeared there, but Neb was too busy glaring at the priests to notice. His hand dropped to the hilt of the curved sword at his waist, which was out of view of the priests, and started to rise when Didu stopped him with a heavy hand on his shoulder.

"What are you doing?"

Nebamun nodded at the priests. "They need to learn some manners."

"Probably. They look like barbarians. But that's not your job."

"Well, I didn't understand what they said, but it sounded like an insult. I know an insult when I hear one."

"You couldn't understand?"

"No, it was some strange language. Maybe Libu. I knew it was an insult from the sound of it."

Didu's eyes widened and he dropped onto the bench, leaning in close to Nebamun. "Are you sure?"

"I'm not close friends with them, if that's what you mean, but they sounded like Libu."

Didu took a casual glance around at the people in the crowded beer hall, hoping there might be some local Medjay they could borrow for assistance, but none were present. The Medjay tended to keep to themselves since they intimidated most of the citizens.

"Neb, if these are Meryey's assassins, we should capture at

least one of them for interrogation. Pharaoh will want to know more. One of us needs to contact the Medjay for help."

Nebamun snorted. "What, for this lot? They don't look like soldiers. If they're the assassins, they're used to sneaking around at night to kill people in their sleep. We can take them, no problem."

"That's not the point. At least one of them needs to stay alive. The Medjay can hold them for a while."

One of the priests staggered backwards and bumped Nebamun's head. He looked down at Nebamun as he righted himself, but he didn't say anything.

"Right. That's enough of that," Neb said. He stood up quickly and broke his empty beer jar over the man's head before punching him in the face. His limp body fell in a heap on the floor.

Didu sighed and lunged past Neb to pound the face of one of the priests into their table. By this time, the largest priest had withdrawn a sword that was hidden in his robes, swinging it toward Nebamun's head. Neb stopped the longer sword with his own, then picked up a bench and swung it to knock the man sideways into a wall. As the priest fell, his sword went through the chest of the priest next to him, who was still struggling to pull his own sword free of his robes.

Having lost his sword in the chest of his friend, the large priest on the floor rolled away under the table. When he stood up, his dagger was in his hand, just inches away from Didu's stomach. Didu jumped backwards to avoid the knife jab as Neb launched himself over the table to land on the priest's back, knocking him to the floor. When Neb stood up, a pool of red was spreading from beneath the fallen priest, who had landed on his own blade.

Nebamun looked down at his handiwork on the floor and shook his head. "I got the clumsy one."

Didu checked the two men that Nebamun had managed not to kill, now lying beside each other. "Two for interrogation. That's not so bad. Judging by their Libu swords and the beards, these could well be the assassins who attacked Hapu's house. They may also have killed the prince."

Nebamun nodded, then grinned. "You think Pharaoh will reward us?"

"Perhaps, but we have to complete our mission first. Even if we know where Hapu is, we still need to find Ray and Prince Ramesses." Didu noticed that they had cleared the beer hall of its customers. "We should probably leave."

"Okay," Neb said, bending over to sling one of the unconscious priests over his shoulder. "I'll get this one. You take the other."

Once Didu had hefted his load, he turned toward the front door of the beer hall, and was startled to see a Medjay patrol following the angry bartender inside. Dressed in their leopard skins, carrying their spears with swords slung from their waists, the Medjay looked impressive. The bartender, probably fearing the wrath of his boss, Panahasi, waved his arms as he told the Medjay how the two ruffians had broken up his beer hall and attacked a group of priests.

The tall Nubian patrol leader, whom the beer hall owner referred to as Nakhtsobek, pointed a well-used spear at Didu and Nebamun. "Put them down. Then drop your weapons."

#

"No! We have to try again!" Ray slapped his hands on Khamenwati's table and stood up from the bench. "My father must not be tortured! He did nothing wrong!"

Khamenwati stood up to place his hand on Ray's shoulder. "He's my friend, and a great teacher. I also want to help him. But we can do nothing now. At sunset, Hapu will lose his nose and ears, but he will survive. Perhaps we can figure out a way to rescue him outside the city when he's on his way to the mines."

Bull continued staring out through the small window at the late afternoon sun. The dust rising from the foot traffic in the street drifted in lazy spirals in the slanting light.

Ray wrung his hands. "We could wait until Hapu is out of the pit. Bull and I could hide near the temple and surprise his guards when Hapu walks past. You could create a distraction."

Khamenwati shook his head. "We tried once already. The Medjay would be ready for another rescue attempt. Hapu would still meet his fate with a strong heart, but that heart would be broken if he knew you were captured as well. It might break his spirit, which is all he has to help him survive right now."

Ray spun around to face Khamenwati. "We can bribe Sermont. Or the mayor."

"I just tried that again. My messenger was turned away. Both Sermont and Mayor Paweraa feel like they're being watched right now, so they would not accept the bribes. To approach the vizier with a bribe would only result in the death of our messenger, and maybe us as well."

"Father," Bull said, still facing the street.

"That would take too long," Ray said. "For now, we have

to assume we have no friends in Pharaoh's golden house, in any case."

"The gods have made their decision, Ray. I'm sorry, but you have to accept that."

"The gods!" Ray banged his fist on the table. "The gods have not helped us at all! They haven't helped Hapu, who is always so careful to make regular sacrifices and pray to them! Even Thoth has abandoned us!"

Khamenwati stared at Ray with wide eyes. "Watch what you say, young man. The gods can hear you. Yes, the gods can make mistakes, but they also know more than we do. The wise Thoth may have decided that Hapu needs to start a new season of his life and learn new things. Or perhaps Hapu is being punished for reasons we can't understand."

"You're a fool if you believe that. We determine our own fates. We have proof that the gods will not help us."

Khamenwati did not take offense. His voice was gentle. "The ways of the gods are beyond our understanding."

Ray snorted. "That's for sure. In any case, I'm leaving. Bull will help me. Stay here if you wish. If we return with Hapu, we won't have much time and we'll need a quick route out of the city. Maybe you'll have some ideas by then."

"I'll do what I can," Khamenwati said, sagging onto the bench.

#

The Hall of Justice was a small building that housed the workplace and barracks of Sermont and his Medjay staff of Nubian and Egyptian officers. A Medjay battle shield hung over the front entrance. A great crowd gathered in the street, speaking in hushed tones and milling about with the occasional glance up to the flat roof of the Hall of Justice. Didu and Nebamun also looked up, but saw nothing as they were hustled through the front door by their Medjay escort.

Inside, a small shrine in the entryway held a statue of the goddess Maat, her head adorned with a white feather of truth.

Sermont was prepared to beat the truth out of Didu and Nebamun as soon as they arrived, but the detainees took the disconcerting approach of immediately telling him the full details of the fight with the priests in the Eye of Horus. They then claimed that they were on a mission from the co-regent, Pharaoh Ramesses III, to hunt down the priests and some escapees from the golden house. Sermont knew this was an outrageous claim, but the criminals were confident in their stories and did not contradict themselves. Sermont would normally beat them at this stage to see if their stories changed, but something about the man named Didu prompted him to consider other means of verification first.

At Didu's direction, Nakhtsobek reached into the linen sack that Didu had carried with him, removing a papyrus scroll bound in leather. The seal of the royal serpent was on the cover, as was the cartouche of Ramesses III. Sermont bit his lip, wondering if he should open the document and glance through it as if he could read, or whether he should just hand it to Nakhtsobek, which seemed like the best solution.

After Nakhtsobek broke the seal, unrolled the first section of papyrus, and scanned it, he frowned at Sermont. "I suggest we let them go. This document is from Pharaoh, and it mentions Didu by name, directing all government officials to aid and support him in his mission."

Sermont scratched his head. This wasn't going quite the way he had planned. "And what mission would that be?"

"It doesn't specify," Nakhtsobek said, scanning the document further. "However, it goes into great detail about the punishments that Pharaoh will deliver upon anyone who obstructs or hinders the bearer of this document or his companions."

"That companion would be me," Nebamun said, looking at Didu. "Where did you get a document like that? We could do anything and get away with it. Free beer, for a start."

"Pharaoh is wise," Didu said. "He foresaw that we would have problems in our search."

"Who, or what, are you looking for?" Sermont asked.

"To start with, those two priests who were still alive," Didu said. "Where are they?"

Nakhtsobek pointed out at the street with his spear. "We left them in the Eye of Horus with one of my men. They were waking up as we left, so I said they were free to go when they were able to walk."

Didu sighed. "I don't suppose they mentioned where they were going?"

"Wherever priests go, I suspect. To their temple?"

"If they were real priests, which they are not, their temple would be in Libu."

At this point, it dawned on Sermont that he might be in deep trouble. He glared at Nakhtsobek. "Fool! You should have held the priests!"

Nakhtsobek's eyes narrowed as he held Sermont's gaze in silence.

Sermont looked away. "You will go with these two royal

servants and act as their guide to the city. If you find the priests, bring them back here for interrogation. If these men desire anything while you're with them, make sure they get it."

"You have a scribe in custody," Didu said. "A man named Hapu. We want him released to our custody before we leave."

Sermont swallowed. "That will not be possible."

Didu drew himself to his full height. "I speak with the authority of Pharaoh."

"I understand, but the great criminal Hapu stands before the abyss of eternity," Sermont said, beckoning them as he turned and stepped onto the stairway leading to the roof. "Follow me."

#

A stout wood stake, about the height of an adult man, stood firmly fixed near the edge of the flat roof in view of the noisy crowd below. The end of the stake had a sharp point. Standing on a small platform behind the stake, facing the crowd with head held high, was Hapu. His arms were held by two big Nubians wearing the leopard skins of the Medjay. To one side, Vizier To and Mayor Paweraa stood as witnesses. Mai, the Scribe of the Place of Examination, was just finishing an explanation to the crowd below that Hapu was to be impaled "on the wood" for trying to escape his original punishment of having his nose and ears cut off. Although the great Vizier To was merciful, Hapu's actions had forced the vizier's hand and tomb robbers could not be tolerated. However, the vizier had opened his heart and taken pity on Hapu, ordering that he be impaled through the torso for a quicker death, rather than the lingering agony of the long pole.

Didu knew his options were limited. He could interfere with the vizier, the second most powerful man in the country, and try to stop the execution in full view of the people gathered below. The vizier would not appreciate defiance of his authority and might not take the time to read Pharaoh's document before ordering Hapu's death and Didu's arrest. He could try to stop the impalement by force, but the Medjay were sure to respond first, and might just kill Didu before explanations could be made. He glanced at Nebamun, who was ready for anything, but there was no time to plan. Then his decision was made for him.

Detecting their arrival on the roof, Hapu looked at Didu, gave him a brief smile as if he recognized him, then lurched free of the Medjay and impaled himself on the stake. The sharp point pierced his chest and protruded a few inches above his shoulder blades. His arms and legs dangled above the roof. He gurgled once and made an effort to raise his head, glancing out at the startled mob for a moment before his body went limp.

A man screamed in the crowd below.

Responding to the vizier's red face and angry glare, the two Medjay guards hastily explained that Hapu had thrown himself on the stake. Didu moved forward to the edge of the roof and looked down on the crowd, where he spotted a young man struggling in the grip of a larger man. The crowd around them backed away to avoid harm. The young man screamed once more before the larger man raised his fist and knocked him out, then carefully picked him up over his shoulder and carried him away. Although they were too far away for Didu to be certain, he thought he recognized the larger man as his quarry—the young Prince Ramesses. Considering his companion's response to the death of Hapu, he could only guess that he must be Ray. Although they seemed friendlier than Didu had been led to believe, there wasn't time to work out the situation or their relationship any further.

"Neb! They're down there!"

Nebamun looked confused, but quickly followed Didu down the stairs. Wanting to look as if he had some control over the situation, Sermont glared at Nakhtsobek and pointed. "Go with them!"

The Medjay guards paid no attention to the commotion, their eyes locked on the angry vizier yelling about how incompetent they were and how he should send *them* to the mines of Timna.

Hapu said nothing. His eyes stared into eternity.

#

After forcing their way through the audience that still milled around gossiping about the dramatic death of Hapu, Didu and Nebamun found themselves stopped behind Nakhtsobek where a warren of narrow passages came together in a busy intersection. In every direction, people stood in the doorways of their homes, or spoke to neighbors in the streets, or hauled goods home from the markets. Golden shafts of light from the setting sun angled through the ever-present dust swirling in the air, which was spiced with the scents of cooking fish and vegetables. It would be another hour before full darkness settled over the city, but Ray and the young prince had vanished into the lengthening shadows. Nakhtsobek sniffed the air like a dog as his gaze swung from one passage to the next.

"Any ideas?" Didu asked.

"It's easy for someone to get lost in the crowd here," said Nakhtsobek. He could see over the heads of most people in the crowd, and his narrowed eyes remained focused on his task.

"So I gathered."

"Do you know where they might go? Is there a familiar place where they would hide?"

Nebamun looked at Didu. "Hapu's house?"

"Too obvious, I think."

Nebamun snorted. "You have a better idea?"

Nakhtsobek pointed. At the end of a long passage directly to the west of them, a commotion had started. At that distance, a large man appeared to be swinging a heavy sack at the heads of two bearded men, and startled onlookers were backing away. Nakhtsobek ran ahead, forcing his way through the unsuspecting citizens in the street. Didu and Nebamun looked at each other, then sprinted into a parallel passage that was less crowded.

#

A bearded priest with a dagger stood a few steps to the left of Bull in a small intersection. To his right, the unconscious Ray was on top of a second priest lying dazed on the ground, his dagger knocked to one side, struggling to get up. The standing priest was larger than Bull, but he warily circled his target as he planned his attack. Unarmed but still big enough at his age to be a threat, Bull growled at the man, his fists clenched, crouched and ready to lunge forward. Around the fringes of the fight, women pulled their children into doorways and men stared in fascination. Bull heard running footsteps approaching, but he didn't want to take his eyes off his adversary. The priest smiled and put his dagger away, confusing Bull for a moment before he pulled the long sword that hung from his belt. Bull considered running into the crowd, but now it would be hard to pick up Ray and leave before the large priest ended his life. With a quick glance, he saw Ray waking up as the priest underneath him rolled his body to one side, then reached for his lost dagger. That was when the great Amun-Re chose to save them.

The large priest twisted as he sensed the approach of Didu, barely raising his weapon in time to block Didu's sword thrust toward his chest. He staggered back and watched as Didu's sword sliced the air where he had been standing, along with a section of his sleeve that fluttered to the ground.

Bull charged toward Ray and hauled him to his feet as Nebamun slammed into the smaller priest, knocking him down again. Spotting the passage that would lead to Khamenwati's school for scribes, he half-carried and half-dragged the stumbling Ray into the shadows.

#

Four days after Itennu's attempted escape, he was still sore from the beating that the skeletal Bai had given him on the dock. He warily watched as Bai and another wetyu dragged a corpse on a sled to the covered entrance of the Place of Purification where Itennu waited. Ay stood next to Itennu with his scribe kit, ready to take notes. Bai kicked the corpse off the sled under the canopy so that the other wetyu could drag it away again. Then he glared at Itennu. "Still sore about your beating?"

Ay cleared his throat. "Tell us about the order, Bai. We have work to do."

Bai spit at the corpse. "Old farmer. No money. The Scribe of the Tomb tried to work a deal with the wife, but she just wants the basics. I said we'd take good care of him. You can throw him in the river for all I care."

"What's his name?" Ay asked.

Bai considered this for a moment, then grinned, displaying his missing teeth. "Wakhakwi."

Ay sighed and shook his head. "I doubt that he was named 'Little Fool.'"

Bai kicked the corpse, still wrapped in threadbare linen. "Look how small and frail he is. And his wife was a fool to think we'd waste any time on him."

Horrified, Itennu took two threatening steps forward to face Bai, barely able to keep himself from hitting the man. "We must have his real name so the gods can find him."

Bai looked at Ay. "What's with the pup? Is he looking for another beating? Haven't you told him we're running a business here?"

Itennu gritted his teeth. "Give us the name!"

Bai reached around behind his back as if to go for the knife they all knew he kept tucked into the waist of his loincloth.

"Is Itennu causing problems again?" boomed the voice of the god, Anubis.

Bai jerked his head around to see Setau standing in the darkness just inside the entrance with his Anubis mask on his head. "I was telling the pup that the man's name was Ashai, my lord. Then he threatened me."

"Itennu! Come here!"

Itennu sighed and walked through the entry into the cooler darkness beyond. Setau towered over him in his mask.

"You've been here almost a month, Itennu. By this time, most novices have adjusted to their new jobs as corpse washers. I know you're not stupid because Ay likes you, but nobody else does. Normally, a month of corpse washing in the Place of Purification brings a clarity of purpose to the new fish, and they want to prove themselves so they can be promoted to better jobs, but I'm not so sure about you. I also know you tried to escape recently, but that's also pretty typical for our recent arrivals. So, here's what I'm going to do. If you can behave yourself for another two weeks and wash corpses without getting into any more fights, I'll talk to Ay about posting you in the drying room instead. I know you've had some training in there, but there's a lot more to learn, and if you're posted to that position, we'll hunt down another candidate to wash the corpses."

Itennu wasn't sure how to respond. As a corpse washer, he felt like he could fight for the dead poor so they wouldn't be allowed to rot after they soaked in the palm wine. He knew Osiris wanted everyone to have a chance at immortality, but there was too much corruption in the system. On the other hand, if he spent more time in the drying room, maybe he could work extra hours to make sure the low-budget jobs received proper attention. They might not be properly mummified, but their bodies would last a lot longer.

"I suppose you're thinking about what happens if you can't behave yourself for two weeks," Setau said. "In that case, you'll be a permanent corpse washer. It's a good way for you to learn humility."

Itennu heard a snort. Out of the corner of his eye, he saw Bai scuttling away from the doorway.

"You may respond," Setau said. "What have you decided?"

Itennu gave his boss a slight bow. "I will do as you ask, my lord. My wish is to serve the Great Osiris the best way I can, and I think that would be in the drying room." Or he could try to run away again if he had a good opportunity, but he couldn't blow it the next time.

"A wise choice. With that settled, let me ask you, have you remembered anything about why Bakenkhons sent you here? I have bets with my personal staff about what you might have done, but nobody gets paid until you tell us."

Itennu shook his head. "I'm sorry, my lord. The blow to my head is all I remember." He remembered perfectly, to be honest, but he wasn't going to tell anyone.

"Hmm. That's unfortunate. You remember nothing about sleeping with the wife of Bakenkhons? Or with his mistress? It would be most helpful if you did, since that's what I'm betting on," Setau said, giving him a little nudge in the ribs with his elbow.

"I'm sorry, my lord."

"How about if I say you don't have to wash corpses any more? If I say you can skip standing in the soft mud with all those disgusting liquids and the rot of the floating dead? Sounds good, doesn't it? A normal person would jump at the chance."

Itennu hesitated, but he knew Osiris was also watching to see what his servant would decide. "If I remember at some point, you'll be the first to know, my lord. Thank you for the offer. I am but dust upon your feet."

Setau sighed heavily, and the sound was amplified inside his mask.

"Back to work, Itennu. I hear we've got a big load coming in that nobody else wants to touch."

Four

1184 BCE—Royal City of Pi-Ramesses

Year 4 of His Majesty, King of Upper and Lower Egypt, Chosen by Re, Beloved of Amun, Pharaoh Setnakhte, Second Month of Akhet (Season of Inundation), Day 28

#

Ramesses stood beside his father's bedside in silence. Shafts of mid-morning sunlight from the high windows cut through the sweet clouds of healing incense that drifted through the room. He had been making daily offerings to Amun-Re, Thoth, and various other gods that could intervene to improve Setnakhte's health, but he sensed that the gods were unhappy with the way Egypt's affairs were being managed right now, so they might keep ignoring his requests for help until maat had been restored to the Two Lands. With Setnakhte unable to perform his daily duties at the Temple of Amun-Re, the dawn greeting and other tasks had been delegated to High Priest Bakenkhons until Ramesses could get caught up on all the other matters that demanded his attention after his long absence. Perhaps the god was mad about that—he either wanted Ramesses to appear in person or, like most people, he didn't like Bakenkhons.

Benanta, his Chief Physician, consulted with Setnakhte's royal physician, Seini, on a daily basis, and they had tried various treatments. Some seemed to help the old pharaoh, but most did nothing to improve his condition. When Setnakhte was lucid, the physicians would summon Ramesses to his bedchamber so that they could talk, but these conversations tended to be very short, and his father mainly seemed concerned with his nightmares about the future of the empire, or his visions of imaginary threats from his own family. While these fears were natural in one who was so old and close to his journey into the western horizon, they were distractions that kept them from discussing more important matters.

Ramesses heard someone clearing his throat in the doorway, and turned to see two men flat on their faces just inside the bedchamber. A tray of food rested on the floor beside them. A guard nodded to him from the doorway.

"You may rise," Ramesses said.

Pantry Chief Paibakamana rose first and bowed again, gesturing at the tray of food being picked up by Court Butler Mastesuria, who was one of the younger members of the staff. Paibakamana wore a gleaming white kilt wrapped around his body, barely containing his soft and formless shape that reminded Ramesses of a melting marsh mallow. In his mid-thirties, he had risen to the post of Pantry Chief after four years of reliable work in the court's kitchens. Ramesses had long suspected that Mastesuria was a child of Thoth because he looked more like a bird than a man. His narrow face and bulging eyes rested atop an unusually tall and thin body. He now held the food tray in his birdlike arms, careful to keep his eyes lowered in respect.

"Does it take two of you to deliver a tray of food?"

Paibakamana smiled and bowed again. "My apologies, Great One. After my staff prepares the food for presentation to His Majesty, Pepi tastes it in the kitchen. The new process then requires myself and a court butler to deliver the food into His Majesty's possession."

"New process? Who ordered this change?"

"Queen Teya, Your Majesty. His Majesty, the good god Pharaoh Setnakhte, may he live a long a prosperous life, has concerns that his food should be carefully watched after it is tasted."

"Ah, I see. Why doesn't Pepi taste it for my father when it arrives in this room?"

"Her Majesty says that the little man annoys the good god when he is here, so he has been banished to the kitchen to perform this duty."

Ramesses considered this information. Pepi was an acquired taste, and one that he had never acquired himself. Pepi had first come to his father's attention before Setnakhte had become pharaoh and was still slaying the rebels and petty local chieftains who had brought disorder to the Two Lands. The little man had distinguished himself in battle against much larger foes, and was rewarded with a posting to his father's personal staff to become his food taster. However, Ramesses had never liked Pepi's attitude, so he could see why Teya had finally tired of his presence. He gestured at the table by Setnakhte's bedside. "Proceed."

"Thank you, Highness."

Ramesses placed his hand on his father's bare shoulder and

gave him a gentle shake. "Father, your food is here. I can feed you, if you wish."

Setnakhte's eyelids fluttered, but his breathing quickly became deeper as he returned to his sleep. Ramesses hoped his dreams were good ones, but wanted his father's advice.

Looking at the food on the tray, Ramesses picked up a fig and smelled its sweet fragrance. His stomach rumbled and he realized it had been many hours since he had eaten breakfast.

There were so many things he needed to discuss with someone, and only one person who was an equal that he could fully trust with his fears, concerns, and hopes. Isis had a good understanding of people, and the motivations of the social climbers among the nobles in the royal court, but she didn't have the knowledge of a pharaoh. Setnakhte had always been good with strategy, which had served him well when he took control of the chaos to rebuild the empire, and there was knowledge he would share with no one other than his oldest son. That was the knowledge that Ramesses needed more of now. His father had focused much of his training on becoming a powerful warrior who could lead men into battle, but the strategies of war did not apply as well to managing the vast empire of the Two Lands. Confrontation and the roles played by the combatants in a battle were very clear, but the vagaries of politics and power and the desires of grasping nobles and bureaucrats who hid behind smiles, whispers, and respectful bows were another matter entirely. Ramesses had learned some of these skills, but Setnakhte had the uncanny ability to understand the delicate political balance between the pharaoh's powers and the disguised agendas of the sycophantic priests who must constantly be watched.

With the foreign incursions into Egypt as other states tested the boundaries ruled by the new pharaoh, there had been little time to pass all of this knowledge from father to son. If Setnakhte's health did not improve, he would be entirely on his own. Yes, he had many advisors, but the most trusted members of his staff were those who had survived the rigors of battle by his side, and they did not have the skills to manage a civilian population. Ramesses also trusted the gods to help him rule, but he had to prove himself capable of managing the country before he could expect their full support. He also needed their help to keep his family safe.

The thought of his own failures with his family's security weakened his knees and forced him to sit on the edge of the bed by his father. Amanakhopshef was dead at the hand of an assassin and not yet safe in his tomb for his journey into the beautiful west. Young Ramesses—the Hawk-in-the-Nest—was still missing and either dead or in the hands of his captors. If Bull never returned, he might eventually have to name Pentawere as his successor. That was Pentawere's right due to his age, but much could happen before then, and others might be a better choice when the time came. These were matters best left unsaid, just as his father had told him. To announce someone as the Hawk-in-the-Nest was to put a target on their back.

The smell of the fig tickled his nostrils.

Pentawere was also old enough now that he should be named to a position of authority where people would learn to respect him as he learned how to command—perhaps he would name him the Commander in Chief of Elite Foot Troops so that he could train with the army and serve directly under him.

Chief General Hori would help train him. If he were to return, Pentawere would serve under Bull since he was the Commander in Chief of the Army—a traditional role for one training to be pharaoh. But these would be matters for happier times when his family was back together.

He should also do his duty and have more children with his wives. Normal children had enough diseases and fatal accidents to worry about, but royal children had to be protected from those who actively wanted to kill them, so it was best to have as many potential successors as possible to maintain the dynasty.

Too many things to think about. He studied the fig in his hand and put it down on the tray. He had lost his appetite.

#

This being the second month of flood season, the strong currents of the Nile kept trying to push the small fishing boat off its course. Khamenwati had a tight grip on both sides of the boat as it bounced along, and he felt nauseous, but Bull was doing a great job of rowing them across the surging waters lit only by the minimal glow of a quarter moon. During the day, the trip from the Theban east bank to the City of the Dead on the west bank was a manageable affair, but the hidden rocks and sand banks they might hit in the darkness made this trip much more exciting.

Ray, however, didn't seem to notice, staring up at the moon as if he were sitting in the garden of his father's house drinking a jar of beer. Khamenwati was worried about the boy. Ever since Bull had returned to his house two nights ago dragging Ray along behind him, the boy had said almost nothing. His students had already informed him of Hapu's sad demise before they arrived, so he had arranged for a hiding place in a secret room adjacent to the Thoth shrine in his scribe school. This secret room was where Khamenwati or his deputy priest would hide to perform the role of oracle when students wanted to ask questions of Thoth, so its location was known only to the two of them. No one had coming looking there for the boys, but his student spies reported that the land and water routes in and out of Thebes were under close watch by the Medjay. He couldn't hide them forever, and he owed it to Hapu to keep his son and his mysterious friend safe. While he suspected that the larger young man was a member of the royal family who needed protection, he knew enough not to ask so that any questioning or torture by the Medjay would not force him to reveal the young man's identity. With the other routes out of the city under observation, that left him with one move to get the boys to safety. He couldn't arrange a boat for a dangerous river crossing at night without explaining why, so Khamenwati had his students locate an unprotected fishing boat away from the city's main landing areas so that he could steal it. Another of his students had made the crossing earlier in the day so that he could row Khamenwati back to the city later that night.

Lost in his thoughts, Khamenwati jumped in his seat when the boat hit a thick patch of reeds on the west bank. As planned, they were well away from the watersteps at the main landing area. Bull stepped out into the water, plunging up to his waist in the strong current, and hauled the boat through the reeds onto the bank. As long as they could avoid the Medjay who patrolled the necropolis looking for tomb robbers every night, they would be able to hide until morning.

Expressionless, Ray stepped onto the muddy bank and helped Khamenwati out of the boat as Bull tied it to a rock. Now came the hard part. He had tried explaining his plan to both of them earlier in their cramped hiding place at the school, but Bull didn't seem to understand what was required, and Ray simply stared at the statue of Thoth in its shrine. He gestured for them to sit down on a group of rocks where the reeds screened them from view.

"All right, boys. We've made it this far, so now you'll have to keep an eye out for the necropolis police. Along the banks and the valley floor, you'll mostly see the Medjay on their chariots, and that means you'll hear their horses before you can see them in the darkness. That should give you time enough to hide unless they've already spotted you, in which case their arrows will find you faster than you can run. The Medjay are legendary for their archery skills, and their bows are powerful enough to hit long-range targets. They're going to assume you're tomb robbers if you're walking around out here at night, so they won't give you any warning—they'll just shoot you if they can see you. Do you understand?"

Bull just blinked at him. Ray stared at the river.

Khamenwati sighed and continued, hoping for the best. "There are plenty of family tombs near the worker's village—the Place of Truth—where you can hide. You may find offerings of food there as well. The Medjay are only interested in robbers hunting for royal tombs. If you can stay hidden for a day or two, you can make your way over the mountain at night when the workers aren't using the path. You'll just have to be quiet and careful to get around the Medjay guard hut at the top of the trail where it starts down into the Great Place. I sometimes take my advanced students there to get experience working for Huy, the Senior Scribe of the Tomb. There are warehouses on the valley floor with tools and food for the tomb workers, but those are well protected so you should stay away from them. After you cross the valley, you can go on up to the desert flatlands above the Great Place. Walk north in the desert for a night or so, and then it should be safe for you to return to the river and find other transportation."

Ray snorted. "And go where?"

Khamenwati smiled. At least Ray was paying attention now. "That's up to you. Get a ride from someone on the river. It's better that I don't know where you might go so that the Medjay can't beat the information out of me."

Ray frowned at Khamenwati. "Do you think that's likely?"

"If they hunt hard enough, someone will make the connection between me and Hapu. When I get back to the city, I'm going to look for Hapu's body anyway to make sure he gets beautified for his journey to meet Osiris. The school can afford it."

"Then maybe you should go with us."

"I'm too old and weak for that kind of an adventure, Ray. And I have my responsibility to my students and the school. I'm just happy that I could get you and your friend to safety. It's what Hapu wanted, and if it was important enough for him to risk his own life to make sure the two of you were safe, I'm sure your friend must also be very important."

Bull plucked a beetle from one of the reeds and ate it.

Ray watched Bull chew on the crunchy beetle. "He is. I'll take care of him."

\#

Khamenwati was correct. The night that they arrived on the west bank, Ray and Bull walked about two miles across the raised causeway above the flooded fields that led from the ferry landing to the towering walls and warehouses of the temple district. The soft moonlight was enough for them to see without making them obvious to any Medjay who might be watching. Keeping to the shadows, they continued past the temples to the trail leading along the base of the cliffs to the worker's village—the Place of Truth.

A perimeter wall surrounded the neat little village built to house the tomb builders, artisans, and water carriers. From their viewpoint on the trail leading to the northern gate, they saw only the roofs of the single-story mud-brick structures that looked like a hive of dozens of homes. The southern slope below the village held the aromatic garbage dump, where defiant rats stopped their feeding to watch them walk past. On the flat area atop the southern slope, cows shuffled in their pens along with the donkeys that protected them from predators. The smell of these animals, mixed with rotting garbage and the lingering scents of grilled fish and spices from evening meals, assailed their nostrils as they got closer to the community. On the higher ground outside the northern wall, a row of eighteen carefully built stone temples housed the gods who kept watch over the village. While these temples were smaller than those elsewhere in Thebes, built of rough stones and mud mortar, the homes for Ptah, Hathor, Thoth, and Pharaoh Amenhotep I—the patron of the village—were large enough to hold many of the village residents on festival days. Ray understood that this was a hot and rough place to live, but it was clear that the royal administration took good care of these elite tomb builders.

Aware that many families would be sleeping on the roofs of their homes where it was cooler, they rested long enough for the villagers to settle in, and then left the trail to circle around behind the temples. Seeing no police patrols, they ascended a short distance up the western slope below the cliffs on the village's west side where the family tombs of the workers were located. Although there were small pyramids and mud-brick chapels scattered across the hills around the village, this was the main cemetery where the workers had been burying their families for hundreds of years. Most of these chapels were dug into the ground to make a vault with a small limestone pyramid on top, and many were decorated with colorful doors and stunning art work. It was a small city of the dead connected by a network of branching paths. Ray and Bull rooted through these dark spaces until they found bread, figs, and beer that a thoughtful family member had left as offerings. The figs were dried out and the bread was hard, but they were able to soften it in the beer and eat a modest meal. The food had been there long enough that the spirit of the tomb's occupant must already have eaten, and Ray said a brief prayer of thanks to the dead so they wouldn't take offense. Continuing their search, they found two more tombs that were open with small amounts of food and a sealed jar of beer that they took with them for later.

The exhausting hike over the western cliffs on the steep trail that the workers used to reach the Great Place took a toll on both of them after the long day. They considered stopping to find a place to hide and sleep overnight, but they figured the

Medjay patrols along the trail would be certain to find them. Ray finally decided that they should rest a while and then blend in with the workers early in the morning on their way to the tombs in the Great Place. They moved well away from the trail onto the rocky hillside and hid in the shadows behind a large outcropping of limestone. From their perch high on the mountain, they heard the distant gurgling of the river, the occasional braying of donkeys, and the screech of night birds hunting for prey. Across the Nile, fires still burned to illuminate the east bank temples, and the flickering flames gave life to the huge figures of the dead pharaohs. Watching the great city of Thebes settling in for the night, they soon fell asleep.

Sometime after dawn, Ray heard voices nearby and woke up, bumping his face against the limestone by his head. Bull was already awake, chewing on a piece of bread. He offered a piece of it to Ray, who accepted the hard crust and peered around the rock outcropping toward the trail. A dozen men were climbing the dusty path, strung along it singly or talking in groups of two.

"Come on," Ray said, beckoning to Bull. "We have to hurry to catch up."

A few minutes later, they slipped in behind the last pair of workers as they walked through the narrow gap between a short section of wall to the right of the trail and an elevated guard tower on the left. Between the wall and the guard post, three broad stone steps began the trail's descent into the Great Place hundreds of feet below. As they approached, a tall, dark Medjay leaned out of the tower to look at them, his long black braids swinging loose past his chest. Ray nodded and the guard disappeared from view.

They dropped back away from the workers on the trail to avoid being noticed, but continued their descent. From there, they could see the big warehouses and a small camp filled with huts on the broad valley floor. Scribes bustled around the buildings as they prepared to disburse and keep records of the copper chisels, leather baskets, oil lamps, and other supplies that the work gangs would need on their way to work deep inside the earth. At the lower end of the valley, a man and a young boy led a string of donkeys loaded with supplies past the guard post just inside the narrow passage that separated the Great Place from the dusty wadi that emptied into the distant Nile. Stopping to sit in the shadows of a limestone outcrop a short distance from the path, Ray and Bull studied the valley as they drank the last sips from their beer jar and considered their next move. With so much activity, Ray figured they had little chance of getting food or water from the warehouses, but they would need something to drink soon. Having no other safe options, he decided they should just rest there in the shadows until later in the day.

#

When something touched his shoulder, Ray woke up and sat bolt upright. A young boy, maybe seven or eight years old, stood over him with a look of concern. "You dead?"

Ray blinked. "No." He quickly looked around and saw Bull snoring softly nearby, flat on his back.

"I'm Ruta," said the boy. "Need drink?"

Ray snatched the water skin that Ruta offered and tried to drink slowly. Then he tapped Bull's foot and handed him the water. Ray knew this was a good sign from the gods—they had sent this boy to keep them alive.

"Thank you, Ruta."

"Why you not carry water?" Ruta asked, sitting down between them in the shadows.

"We ran out. We're new here."

"Here to rob tombs?"

Ray was startled by the question. "Oh, no. We're just...looking for work."

Ruta cocked his head with a slight smile. "It's okay. You tell me."

"No, really, we're just looking for work." Ray found this kid disturbing.

"I work here. I bring supplies. Sometimes I get dull chisels from tunnels. I take for sharpening and scribe pay. You painter? You look weak like artist."

Ray wasn't sure if he should be offended. "Yes."

Ruta pointed at Bull and gave Ray a knowing nod. "He cut stone."

"You're right." Better not to tell him the truth. Ray drank more water.

"Need food?"

"You have food?" Ray realized he was smiling.

"No. Funeral near. Food there. Come."

Ruta stood up and started down the path. Ray scrambled to get up and bring Bull along. The gods were watching over them, but he didn't know which one to thank. Probably Hathor, since this was her necropolis and she was also Goddess of the Western Mountain. He would leave an offering for Hathor at his next opportunity.

Following Ruta along a little used trail that wound around

the lower end of the valley and then back across the base of the western cliffs, they eventually came to the site of a royal tomb being built for Pharaoh Setnakhte. As they approached, Ruta explained that it was actually the tomb of Queen Twosret that was now being hastily modified for the living god. What seemed odd was the funeral tent, an empty funeral sled tied to two oxes, and one bald priest in dirty white pleated robes seated on the edge of the sled looking bored. Nobody else was around.

Ruta waved at the priest as they approached, then smiled at Ray. "My friend. He feed us."

Ray's mouth filled with saliva as he saw the wide variety of food displayed on tables below the funeral tent. Bull also walked faster.

When they were about to enter the tent, the priest stood up and tipped his head to the side. "Ray?"

Ray tore his gaze away from the food and looked at the priest. It was Itennu, the young priest he knew from Pi-Ramesses. "Itennu? How are you here?"

Itennu shrugged. "I upset the wrong people."

Bull ignored both of them and started eating figs from the closest bowl on the table. Ray just stared at Itennu, not knowing what to say.

Ruta filled a jar of beer and handed it to Ray. "Drink."

"You better hurry," Itennu said. Everyone is down inside the tomb right now to finish the ceremony, but they'll be back soon for the feast."

"Who died?"

"Osirified Royal Scribe Inyotef, Steward to the living god Pharaoh Setnakhte—life, prosperity, and health. The living god honors his much-loved steward by placing his beautified body in a side chamber of his tomb where he will serve the Pharaoh for eternity."

Ray finished a long drink of the cool beer, nearly draining the jar. "This tomb was built quickly." Ray grabbed a handful of dates and stuffed them in his mouth.

"Not really. This was the tomb of the great criminal Queen Twosret. The tomb the workers were digging for the living god had to be stopped when they accidentally broke into the ancient tomb of Osirified Pharaoh Amenmesse. Since the living god may need his tomb soon, the work switched to this one."

Bull was working his way down the row of bowls on the table, now eating some grilled fish. Ray intended to follow his lead. "Thank you for this food, Itennu."

"It looks like you need it more than the funeral party does. We have more food than they will require, in any case."

Chewing on some kind of roasted bird, Ruta sat on the edge of the funeral sled that had been used to haul the sarcophagus of the scribe out to this remote valley. "He will help."

"Help with what?" Itennu asked.

Ray cleared his throat and moved closer to Itennu so he could speak softly. At close range, he noted an unpleasant smell from Itennu that he couldn't quite define. He hesitated a moment, but decided to trust this priest with their lives. "We told the boy we're looking for work, but we actually need more than that."

Ruta started climbing the packed dirt ramp across the field of limestone chips dumped from the tomb. Ray knew that when the expansion of the tomb was completed and the Pharaoh was placed in his eternal home, the debris and the ramp would be removed to hide its location.

Ray outlined the situation for Itennu, who understood their predicament right away. "Thank you for telling me this, Ray. Those of us who are toys of the powerful need to help each other. I may have a solution for you, but you may not like it and you will have to be patient. I'm sure you will also need the approval of Prince Ramesses, of course."

Ray sighed and explained what had happened to Bull. While he hoped Bull would eventually recover, all they could do was to protect him until then.

Itennu watched Bull devour a small stack of honey cakes. "This saddens me. I do not know the prince, but many spoke of his great promise as the Hawk-in-the-Nest."

After Itennu outlined his plan, Ray sighed heavily and looked at Bull, who was happily drinking another jar of beer. He couldn't say he was happy with Itennu's plan, but they didn't have any better options, and it would be the best way to protect Bull.

The sound of chanting deep within the earth prompted Ruta to turn and wave at them. "They're coming!"

#

Ray and Bull found themselves back in western Thebes, but now they had sunk to the level of becoming corpse washers in the House of Beauty. On the long walk back from the Great Place, Itennu had filled them in on his own recent events from the time he angered High Priest Bakenkhons through his lowly journey as a corpse washer. This exchange reassured Ray that he was trusting the right person, and prompted him to share more details about the events that had brought them there. He was also saddened to hear the news of Prince Amanakhopshaf's arrival at the House of Beauty, and it dredged up the awful memory of his blood-soaked body on the bed.

They were introduced to Itennu's boss, Ay, a short and chubby man dressed in a loincloth who wheezed when he walked. Ray observed that Ay had a tendency to rub the wispy black hair on his head when he was talking, His face was very pale, but Ray assumed that was because the man rarely left the dimly lighted chambers of his employment. Itennu told Ay that Ray and Bull were down on their luck and looking for new careers working with the dead.

Ay chuckled, and that started a hacking cough. When his coughing fit stopped, he nodded at Itennu. "Smart boy. You can't fool old Ay. You brought new recruits to be corpse washers so that Setau will let you work in the drying room instead of spending the rest of your career in this watery nightmare."

Ray perked up. "What?"

Itennu looked at Ray, winked, and briefly shook his head. "Yes, Ay. They're desperate young men. They're perfect for this place because they have no other options, and the Medjay are looking for them."

Ray's heart sank. Had he been betrayed?

"Perfect," said Ay. "They'll fit right in. Don't worry, lads, you'll be safe. We're all criminals here, although some are worse than others."

As Ay and Itennu introduced them to the disgusting tasks of a wetyu and showed them the corpse washing pool, a tall man wearing an Anubis mask over his head glided up to them. While Ray was used to seeing priests dressed as gods, the man had a presence that dominated the room, and a booming voice to match.

"I am Setau, Overseer of the Mysteries, First Prophet of Osiris in Thebes, and your lord for as long as you serve here in the *Per-Nefer*, the House of Beauty. I see you are new. We are in the chambers of the *Wabet*—the Place of Purification, and I will be your--"

Ay gave Setau a dismissive wave. "Yes, yes, we told them all that, my lord."

Setau stopped and cleared his throat. "I see. And what brings the two of you here? I don't want any disruptive influences among my staff. This is a sacred place where we all have a great responsibility, and positions here are not available to just anyone who walks through the gate."

Itennu started to say something, but Ay touched his arm. "They'll be fine. They're running from the police, and they're anxious to learn. Isn't that right, Anu?" Ay looked at Ray significantly and waited.

Ray sighed. "Yes. I am Anu, and I also know how to read and write."

"Really?" Setau leaned back, apparently surprised.

"He's lying," said Ay, glaring at Ray. "He knows a few words, but not enough to paint the prayers and wisdom of Thoth on coffins, if that's what you're thinking, my lord. Itennu warned me that he might lie."

Setau grunted and rotated his massive head to look at Bull, who was bent over to stare at his rippling reflection in the corpse pool, "And what about him? Can he write?"

"That one can't even talk," Ay said. "His name is Montu."

"Montu!" barked Setau. "Pay attention when I speak to you!"

Bull continued staring at his reflection. Ay tapped the side of his head. "He's simple, but we can show him what to do."

"Face in water," Bull said.

Before Setau could comment, Ay leaned toward Setau and broke into a coughing fit. Setau took two steps back. When Ay was done, he cleared his throat. "I'll get them started, my lord."

"Do what Ay says and we won't have any problems," Setau said. "I'll be watching you. And Itennu, if these two work out, you can start your job in the drying room very soon."

Itennu bowed deeply. "Thank you, my lord. That is my greatest wish."

After Setau left, Ay squinted at the three of them. "I hope you like the dead. You're going to meet a lot of them."

\#

In the span of a few weeks, Khait's world changed. As a special treat for her successes with her dancing and the visions sent by Hathor, Shepsit now wanted to teach her how to serve the goddess in the chapel at Hatshepsut's mortuary temple. Since the Opet Festival was over, the priestesses had returned Hathor to her shrine in the chapel, so the visitors were returning with their offerings, questions, and requests.

Just before dawn, Khait lay face-down on the cool stone floor beside Shepsit to start the daily greeting of Hathor. After the greeting, the senior priestesses who were now lying prostrate behind them in the chapel would dress Hathor in clean clothes and provide the goddess with food. Rising to her feet, Shepsit opened the curtains of the sanctuary where Hathor resided and stepped back in a low bow, her arms outstretched with palms up, and began the chant:

\#

Lady of names in the Two Lands,
Unique One.
Lady of terror among the guardian gods,
the Uraeus on the horns of Atum.
The gods come to You prostrating,
the goddesses come to You bowing their heads.
Your father Amun-Re adores You,
His face rejoices in hearing Your name.
Thoth satisfies You wth His glorifications,
and He raises His arms to You, carrying the sistrum.
The gods rejoice for You when You appear.
You illuminate the Two Lands with the rays of Your eyes.
The South, the North, the West, and the East
pay You homage, making adorations to You.
Hathor, Lady of Iunet,
Your beautiful face is pleased by the King of Upper and Lower
Egypt.

\#

Later that morning, after the senior priestesses rubbed Hathor with scented oils and provided her with new clothes, they removed the food offerings and closed the curtains of the shrine. All the priestesses then left the chapel, except for one who remained outside in the farther hypostyle hall to meet the day's visitors lined up to visit Hathor. Clouds of myrrh incense filled the chapel from the burning braziers. Khait now found herself hidden in the candlelit stairwell below the shrine with

Shepsit, who demonstrated how the stairwell made their voices deeper and louder while providing an echo that made people think the goddess was speaking.

As Khait learned more of the temple mysteries, her feelings about this new knowledge became more complex. The visions that Hathor had sent her during her dances were powerful and vibrant, bestowing wisdom she could not have gained any other way. They had a reality about them that felt different from dreams. She still didn't know enough to fully interpret her visions, but Shepsit often reminded her that understanding would come with time. Was this magic, or did the dances reveal deep knowledge already stored within her heart?

Aside from her visions, learning to be an oracle appeared to be trickery.

Since visitors were not allowed to enter the chapel itself, the first woman knelt and placed her forehead on the floor just outside the chapel door. She would have given her offering to the priestess stationed nearby. From her bowing position, she spoke a short prayer and then asked if Hathor would bless her with another child, having lost her first two children to illness.

Shepsit spoke with a breathy voice, drawing out the single word, "Yeeessss."

Delighted, the woman walked away. Khait looked at Shepsit. "How did you know?"

Shepsit shrugged. "I didn't, but there were only two possible answers."

"You lied to her?"

"I am guided by Hathor. Whether my answer is right or wrong, it is Hathor's will. If we told that young woman she would not have another child, Hathor knows her world might be destroyed. Instead, that woman left feeling good about herself and the goddess, which is the best result we can hope for. She will continue to bring offerings."

Khait considered Shepsit's reasoning, but still felt skeptical. "Is that what this is about? The offerings?"

"The temple must survive. Other temples do the same thing, but they're more aggressive about it. The people bring us food, beer, wine, precious stones, and other valuable items. Or they may visit our small market outside the temple to purchase symbolic offerings like figurines or cloths painted with images of Hathor in her cow form. We accept these offerings and then return them to the market to sell them again. We do not have vast farmlands to support us like the cult of Amun-Re, even though Hathor has many followers. If Hathor were to stop using her oracular powers, her followers would stop coming here. The goddess needs followers, just as her followers need the goddess."

They were interrupted by the sound of a young man's chanting voice.

#

Let me worship the Golden One to honor her Majesty,
and exalt the Lady of Heaven.
Let me give adoration to Hathor,
and songs of joy to my heavenly Mistress!
I beg her to hear my petitions
that she send me my mistress now!
And she came to see me!
What a great thing that was when it happened!
I rejoiced, I was glad, I was exalted,

from the moment they said,
"Oh, look at her!"
and "See, here she comes!"
and the young men bowing through their enormous passion for her.
Let me consecrate breath to my Goddess
that she give me my Love as a gift!
It is four days now I have prayed in her name;
let her be with me today!

#

Khait looked at Shepsit, who prodded her shoulder and nodded.

Khait shrugged and shook her head. The silence dragged on. For some reason, her vision of Ray diving into the river popped into her head, distracting her for a moment.

The young man spoke again. "O Golden One, please give me an answer. Will you send my love to be with me today?"

Khait sighed. Imitating Shepsit's voice, she drew out her one word response, "Yeeessss."

"Seven times seven times I fall at your feet, Most Beautiful Lady of the Two Lands! I kiss the earth in reverence to you in all your forms, and to the greatness of your name!"

As they listened to the young man's receding footsteps, Shepsit put one arm around Khait's shoulders and gave her a hug. "You see how happy you made that young man?"

"Yes, but what if his love doesn't visit him today?"

"Then he will assume he did something during the day to offend Hathor, or that he did not give thanks with sufficient offerings, and he will come back to repair his relationship with the goddess. If his love does visit him today, and it makes him happy, he will return with offerings of thanks to ensure that she will see him again. This demonstrates the power of the gods. Hathor also has the powers of the divine female. We must all offer reverence to Hathor, otherwise she may seek revenge on us as Sekhmet."

That made sense to Khait. "And that's why we have the Festival of Drunkenness."

"Yes, and all the other festivals that include Hathor. She teaches us to love and dance and enjoy our short lives in appreciation of her wisdom, otherwise she will kill us."

Khait felt conflicted, as though she were learning too much about the mysteries. She could understand why the temple operated in a way that would help it survive, and why the mysteries were kept from the common people as forbidden knowledge, but it somehow felt wrong to manipulate Hathor's followers. Or was it manipulation? Maybe Hathor really was telling her oracles what to say in her chapel. The gods were too powerful and their actions were beyond human understanding. That's why pharaohs, the living gods, had to communicate with the great gods and then tell their people how best to serve them. Pharaohs had a special relationship with the gods that the temple oracles and high priests would never have, and the people needed their leadership. Or was that another form of manipulation? What if a pharaoh were more human than divine and they decided to lie about the wishes of the gods to benefit themselves? But no, that couldn't happen. Their hearts would be weighed against the Feather of Truth after they died, and their lies would cause their hearts to be eaten by the Devourer, sending them to oblivion. No one wanted to risk that—least of all a pharaoh.

Khait shook her head. Best not to think about it too much. Such thoughts could lead to madness.

#

While Bull moved corpses from the cooling room to the pool of palm wine for cleaning, Itennu brought Ray into the drying room where the body of Prince Amanakhopshaf rested on a slanted stone table along the west wall. White natron salts were scattered around the table and huge gray mounds of used natron rested nearby on the floor. Braziers around the room burned incense to form a thick and flagrant cloud lit from below by the flickering of oil lamps. Setau stood at the head of the corpse wearing his Anubis mask, pleated white robes, and a gold collar as he supervised the work of two sem-priests crowded around the table. All three of them wore their formal leopard skins draped over their robes. A bald figure in white stood silhouetted in one corner by a brazier burning behind him.

Watching the sem-priests do their work, Itennu quietly described the activity for Ray. The *Hetemu Netjerm*, the Sealer Bearer of Osiris, stacked coils of wide linen strips at the end of the table for the wrapping process. The *Hery Heb* softly mumbled spells and prayers while he lined up a series of gold covers for the toes and fingers. The body had completed its drying process for forty days. The torso had been washed with palm wine, cinnamon, and other aromatic spices before being packed with resin-soaked linen that would firm up the body cavities. The face was padded with linen under the eyelids and inside the cheeks. Now, frankincense and myrrh mixed with cedar oil, Syrian balsam, and oil of Libu were being poured over the entire body two times by Setau.

As he poured the oil, Setau's deep voice, echoing inside his Anubis mask, filled the chamber. "Thou hast received the perfume which shall make thy members perfect. Thou receivest the source of life and thou takest the form of it to give enduring form to thy members; thou shall unite with Horus in the Great Hall. The unguent cometh unto thee to fashion thy members and to gladden thy heart, and thou shalt appear in the form of Re; it shall spread abroad the smell of thee. Thou receivest the oil of the cedar in Amentet, and the cedar that came forth from Osiris cometh unto thee."

"Setau loves to perform when he has an audience," Itennu whispered. "The wetyu would normally be doing this work, but that man in the corner is a royal scribe sent here to monitor the process. The sem-priests are actually doing their jobs for once instead of letting us handle it."

The *Hery Heb* began wrapping the prince's head with the linen bandages, keeping them tight to reveal the contours of the face, twice around the top of the head, twice around the mouth, four times around the neck, and so on as Setau forcefully spoke the next prayer.

"Grant thou that breathing may take place in the head of the deceased in the underworld, and that he may see with his eyes, and that he may hear with his two ears, and that he may breathe through his nose, and in the underworld."

As the wrapping continued, Ray remembered how Amana's body had looked when Ray discovered him dying in his bed covered in blood. He tried to force the image from his mind, thinking how much better Amana was going to look when the mummification process was complete. Then a new thought occurred to him.

Ray turned to whisper into Itennu's ear. "We didn't talk about Pentawere. Did his body arrive along with Prince Amanakhopshaf?"

Itennu looked at him and tipped his head to one side. "He would have to be dead to require our services."

Ray swallowed. He felt short of breath. He was certain that Pen had drowned in the Nile in his attempt to save them after they left Pasai's house during the night. He had died to distract the assassins as Hapu, Bull, and Ray escaped in the stolen boat for their long journey to Thebes. "He's not dead?"

"Not that I've heard. Of course, we don't get the most current news here, but the important people always come here to be beautified. We haven't seen him."

Ray tried to explain the situation when they had last seen Pen in the river.

"There's an easy explanation for that. If he drowned, the body was probably eaten by crocodiles."

Ray remained silent for a moment. Itennu's explanation made sense, but something felt wrong about it. Pasai or someone would have made certain that a search for the prince was conducted. The river was big, of course, and fast, and the incident had happened at night, but some trace of Pen's body would likely show up along the riverbank. Assuming it was identifiable when found, the golden house would have retrieved it for proper beautification. If not, the body might not have been buried, and Pen would have experienced the eternal oblivion of the Second

Death. Ray shuddered. Was it possible that Pen had survived after all?

"I think I need to lie down," Ray said, steadying himself with one hand against the wall.

Setau's Anubis head turned toward them. "Wetyu Itennu! If he's going to vomit, get him out of here! We don't want this sacred room defiled!"

Itennu led Ray back into the cleaning room where Bull was washing corpses in the pool of palm wine and sat him down on a stone bench. "I hope you're okay. I wanted them to see us in there. The rest of the wrapping and beautification process for Prince Amanakhopshaf will continue, so the royal scribe will be staying around to monitor things. And that means the bosses are all tied up with the ritual work they normally lay off on the rest of us. With you and Bull here, I think we have a rare opportunity."

"Opportunity?"

Itennu leaned close to whisper in Ray's ear. "I think we can escape."

#

With a jar of beer in his left hand, balancing an armload of figs, radishes, dates, and bread, Nebamun studied the array of foods on the table and finally decided on a spiced Nile perch stuffed with toasted bread for his main dish. Didu watched him wrestle the pile of food through the crowd and back to the low table where they were sitting. A pleasant young woman wearing only a colorful blue beaded collar stepped lightly over to the table to collect the six empty beer jars before Nebamun pushed them off to clear enough room for his food.

Nebamun smiled at the young woman as she bent toward him to collect the jars. Her long black hair, weighted at the end of each narrow braid, swung forward to brush against his arm. As she walked away, Nebamun sighed and looked at Didu. "I love this place. The House of Kifi deserves its reputation. How could any other business compete with this?"

Didu looked at the crowd of men in the room talking, drinking, and watching the many young women who danced and served for their pleasure. Many of them were bearded traders in strange clothes from other lands looking for the best entertainment Thebes had to offer. "Are you thinking about your future again?"

"You talked me out of being a slave trader. I'm thinking that Pi-Ramesses needs a place like this. Something high class, with wine to attract the royal court and the bureaucrats, and good beer for the common people. Maybe with a tree-shaded bathing pool in a private garden out front. A brothel-and-bath-and-beer business. Our friends in the army will love it, but they'll have to behave themselves—no fighting allowed. And I'll get everyone's attention by making it the best brothel in town with exotic and classy women; not like those seedy places near the docks. I'll have good food like this place, and my slaves and servants will keep it clean and organized. And I'll pay everyone well—except for the slaves, of course—so they won't go off and start another business like mine."

"You're assuming Pharaoh doesn't keep us in the army and send us off to a remote border fort because we failed to recover his son and his kidnappers."

Nebamun sighed. "Well, yes, there's that. When is Nakhtsobek going to get here? It'll be dark soon and we've lost almost three days. Not that I'm complaining. I'd live in this place if I could." He stuffed a handful of fish into his mouth.

"I'm sure his Medjay are doing everything they can. He'll come when he has their reports."

"Sounds like a cushy job, working for the police. You eat regularly, you walk around glaring at people, sometimes you get to beat up criminals, and everyone fears you." Nebamun emptied his jar of beer and looked around for the serving woman.

Didu snorted. "Doesn't sound much different from army life."

"Except for the long marches in the heat and choking dust, the threat of death, the bad food, tiresome military drills, the constant smell of sweaty men, and all the rules."

"A fair point, but I still wouldn't want to work for the police."

The crowd parted to let the towering figure of Nakhtsobek through to their table. As he sat down, a servant immediately brought three jars of beer, bowed, and backed away.

Nebamun took one of the jars and nodded to Nakhtsobek. "I see we'll get faster service with you here."

Nakhtsobek grunted, drank his beer, then set down his empty jar and stared into it. "I don't have good news. My men have searched the city, but all we've learned is that a fisherman's boat was stolen two nights ago. They've also been searching any boats traveling past on the river."

"Has it been recovered?" Didu asked.

"That's the strange thing. The fisherman didn't report it to us because the thief returned his boat. They just returned it to a different dock."

"So someone took his boat across the river and came back.

That doesn't sound like the people we're looking for," Nebamun said.

"Unless they had help," Didu said, rubbing his face. He was hoping to report some kind of progress to his superiors. "Have your men searched the west side of the river?"

"They just started over there today, but the regular necropolis patrols haven't seen anything. Most of my men have been focused here in the city or watching the river. It's a big place. Takes a long time to search."

"We can't wait around any longer. We'll move to the west side and help with the search. If they're over there, I assume there are only a few places they can hide."

Nakhtsobek snorted. "There are plenty of places to hide, but my men keep a close watch on the valleys and the hills. Unless they're hiding in one of the temples or the warehouses, they'll need to steal food from family tombs or buy it from an offering stand, so there's a good chance someone will see them."

"Do you have someone in charge over there that we can contact?" Didu asked.

"You can contact me. Sermont is sending me to the House of Beauty to deliver a message to a priest from Pharaoh Setnakhte."

Didu nodded. "We might as well start our search there, then."

Nakhtsobek caught the eye of the serving woman and signaled for more beer. "The good news is that your prey is trapped if they're hiding across the river."

"Unless they escape into the desert," Nebamun said, picking at the remains of his food.

Nakhtsobek shook his head. "That won't happen, but I'll post extra guards in the hills above the Great Place. They'll have to travel light, without supplies—a donkey would slow them down too much. If they still get through somehow, the desert will take care of our problem for us. The desert is death."

#

"So we'll head into the desert," Itennu whispered, handing Ray and Bull hooded sem-priest cloaks to match the one he had stolen from the laundry pile. They stood in the dark passage that led from the cooling pool to the front entrance of the wabet. "Nobody will think to look for us there. Then we can work our way to the Nile and back to Pi-Ramesses to get all of our problems sorted out. I can go into the golden house ahead of you and explain what happened."

"What about the high priest who sent you here?" Ray asked softly.

Itennu shrugged, keeping his eyes on the entrance. "I'll figure something out. Bakenkhons won't know I'm missing for a while, and he might be in Thebes. I can try explaining what happened to my former superior, Merubaste. You can contact him for me, then tell me when it's safe to meet with him. I'm not sure if he likes me, but when he hears how the high priest's behavior with Queen Teya threatens the security of the temple, I'm sure he'll help."

"That sounds like a dangerous plan," Ray said. "Maybe we should talk to someone in the golden house first."

"It may be dangerous, but it's better than staying here."

Ray knew he'd probably decide to help Itennu escape from this prison of the dead, but he kept trying to think of other options. He kept wondering what his father would suggest, and that sad thought reminded him of his loss. His main goal was to keep Bull safe, but maybe continuing to run was not a solution. Itennu's help created new possibilities. Maybe he could find Pasai or someone else in the golden house who would help Ray understand what had really happened. Or if Itennu could get to Queen Isis, perhaps she would help. And if Pen was actually alive and back home, he must have already sorted everything out. Perhaps if Ray could keep any more assassins from finding Bull, the help he needed was actually back where they started, just waiting for their return.

"Okay," said Ray, helping Bull put on his cloak and pull the hood over his head. "Let's do it. How will we get out of the Great Place at night when the Medjay are watching for tomb robbers?"

"The tomb of the living god Pharaoh Setnakhte—may he live a long life of prosperity and health—is still under construction. It was built for Queen Twosret originally, but they removed her and the workmen needed more air for their tomb modifications, so they re-opened the ventilation shaft that climbs to the desert plateau above the Great Place. The boy, Ruta, told me about it. He seems to know a lot of secrets about the tombs. Then I actually saw the shaft when we were preparing Royal Scribe Inyotef's burial chamber. It's steep, but we can climb it. I'm bringing rope in case we need it."

They heard snoring from the entrance. It was dark except for one flickering oil lamp just inside the passage. Itennu picked up a long coil of rope and gestured for Ray and Bull to follow him. They stepped softly along the passage until they could creep past the door guard slumped on the ground by the doorway—a priest that Itennu knew had a reputation for drinking on duty.

When they were a few yards away, they heard the guard's sleepy voice. "Who's there?"

Itennu turned and waved. "It's okay."

Seeing that they were wearing the cloaks of sem-priests, the guard nodded and waved. "Okay."

Ray felt his heart pounding. He was more worried about Itennu being caught than he was about himself, but the moonless darkness of the broad streets between the temples and warehouses seemed full of threats. He and Bull had evaded the Medjay here once before, but he prayed to Thoth that they wouldn't find them tonight out in the open. The gods might want to punish them for sneaking through the sacred precincts of the City of the Dead a second time. You could never predict what the gods would do. Despite keeping to the shadows when they neared the braziers lighting the entrances to the temples, they had only been walking a short time when a nasal voice called out to them. "Hey! Where are you going?"

Itennu glanced at Ray. "Don't turn around. Just keep walking. I'll handle Bai."

Ray and Bull were approaching the fork in the path to the worker's village when Itennu caught up to them again.

"He let you go?" Ray asked.

"Not exactly," Itennu said. "When he saw who I was, he was going to yell for help. We've had problems before, and I was afraid that he'd draw the attention of the Medjay, so I had to keep him quiet. We have enough time to get away now."

"What did you do?"

"Let's just say I no longer have the rope."

Five

1184 BCE—Thebes

Year 4 of His Majesty, King of Upper and Lower Egypt, Chosen by Re, Beloved of Amun, Pharaoh Setnakhte, Third Month of Akhet (Season of Inundation), Day 1

#

"They beat me, tied me up, and left me for dead right out there in the street!" Bai screamed, hopping from foot to foot in agitation next to the cooling pool in the Place of Purification. "After I woke up, I didn't think I'd live through the night! You don't know how dangerous it is out there at night! They are dangerous criminals who must be executed!"

Didu looked at Nebamun and rolled his eyes. Nakhtsobek was poking around the dimly lit room with his nose wrinkled in disgust. The smell of the place wasn't as strong as Didu had anticipated, but the scent of palm wine and various kinds of sweet incense drifting in from other chambers wasn't enough to mask the distinct odor of decay. Three bodies floated in the gurgling waters of the cooling pool like drowning victims. With his skeletal body, missing teeth, and dirty loincloth, Bai looked like he belonged in the cooling pool with the other corpses. Perhaps he was just a spirit who hadn't realized he was already dead.

"Your Medjay patrols are blind and deaf! I didn't see one of them come by all night while I was out there yelling my head off!"

That got Nakhtsobek's attention. He spoke through gritted teeth as he walked closer to tower over Bai. "You will be quiet now unless you're answering our questions."

Bai sniggered and took a step closer to Nakhtsobek, glaring into his eyes. "I'm not telling you anything else, tough guy. I already told you who attacked me—Itennu, Anu, and Montu. Go do your job."

Nakhtsobek stood perfectly still, looking at Bai with dead eyes. "Where did they go after they tied you up?"

Bai tried to shove Nakhtsobek, but it looked like he was pushing against a giant rock. Bai then found himself bent over the corpse pool looking at his own reflection with one arm twisted up behind his back. "Let go of me! I told you I'm not helping you! It was you Medjay who put me here in the first place!"

"I'm going to explain things to you, Bai. Itennu has been summoned to the golden house, which means he's under our protection. The other two that he's with are of interest to my friends here. They've come a long way and they aren't going to be as patient with you as I am. Do you understand?"

Bai wriggled in his grip. "I look forward to seeing you here soon on one of my tables, Medjay! I have something special in mind for your corpse!"

Nakhtsobek plunged Bai's head into the water and held it

there. When he noticed the small knife sticking out of Bai's waistband at the small of his back, he flicked it into the mud.

Nebamun turned away. "Gods. That is disgusting."

"You have a better idea?" Didu asked.

Nebamun tapped the hilt of the dagger in his belt. "This can be very convincing. Just one or two little stabs would make him talk."

Nakhtsobek raised the spluttering Bai's head just above the water. "I'll ask again, Bai. Where were they going?"

Bai kept spitting into the water. "How would I know that? You think we sat around and had a beer together before they left? Ay might have known!"

"And where is Ay now? I want to talk to him."

Bai awkwardly gestured at the one of the floating corpses with his free hand. "He's right there! He's not going to say much, though. He died this morning. Itennu probably killed him! There was something funny going on between those two."

Setau stepped into the room holding his Anubis mask under one arm. "Ay started his journey to the western horizon during the night. He has been very ill. What is going on here?"

Nakhtsobek held his grip on the struggling Bai, who now looked hopeful that he was about to be rescued. "This is police business, and these two men were sent by Pharaoh. We have questions and your man is not cooperating with us."

Setau nodded and gave them a dismissive wave of his hand. "Yes, that sounds like Bai. Please continue."

"I hope the Devourer eats your heart!" Bai yelled as his head plunged into the water once again.

"Can I get you gentlemen any refreshments? We have beer

and some wine. Or perhaps some honey cakes? My assistant just made them for our visitor from the royal court. Beautification is tiring work, and Prince Amanakhopshaf is receiving the best possible care. You can tell that to the royal family if anyone should ask."

Didu and Nebamun both declined. Nakhtsobek was too busy holding the struggling Bai underwater to answer.

"Do you have any idea where Itennu and the others might have gone?" Didu asked.

"Well, Itennu won't be coming back here; I can assure you of that. He knows he'll be punished for escaping. And I don't think he'll go to Thebes or to Pi-Ramesses because High Priest Bakenkhons will be looking for him once he learns that he escaped from our care. I don't mind telling you I'm a little concerned about that. The High Priest can be vindictive."

Ray tipped his head. This was interesting news. "The High Priest sent him here? Do you know why?"

Setau chuckled. "Itennu said he couldn't remember. Smart boy. Personally, I suspect Itennu was caught traveling in the marshes with the wife of the High Priest. It has certainly happened before, and you'd know why if you ever met her. The High Priest is a lucky man, but he should keep a short leash on her, if you know what I mean."

Didu considered the new information about Itennu, and he wondered what the relationship might be between Itennu, Prince Ramesses, and Ray. He didn't know why the golden house wanted to speak with Itennu, but it was an unusual summons and Nakhtsobek had also been directed to protect the young priest. This indicated that Itennu was not suspected to be one of the kidnappers, so it raised questions as to why he was helping Ray, and why the young prince had not escaped from his captors. Based on the description he'd been given, and vague memories of seeing Ray at the golden house with the princes, the boy was too spindly to keep Prince Ramesses from running away if he chose to do so.

"Bai said the others were Anu and Montu. Is that correct? And what did they look like?"

The description that Setau provided sounded like their fugitives. Then Setau shrugged. "As to their names, who can say? Names don't really matter much here. I suspect half of my staff has never given us their real names. We are all servants under the watchful gaze of Anubis and Osiris, and they know the truth in our hearts."

Bai was struggling less now. Nakhtsobek lifted him out of the water so he could gasp for air. "Do you remember anything now, Bai?"

"No! A million times a million times I say no!" Bai spit something glutinous out of his mouth.

Nebamun looked at Didu. "I'm starting to think he doesn't know anything."

"Better to be certain," Nakhtsobek said, slowly lowering Bai's face toward the water again.

"They were walking toward the cliffs! I don't know if they were going to the worker's village or if they took the trail up the wadi to the Great Place."

Nakhtsobek pulled Bai back away from the water and dropped him on the mud. "See there, Bai? See how much better you feel now that you've gotten that off your chest? Is there anything else you want to tell us?"

Bai rolled on his back, staring up at Nakhtsobek with a mixture of fear and hatred in his eyes. He kept quiet and shook his muddy head back and forth several times.

"It sounds like we need to split up and move quickly," Didu said. "Nebamun and I can take the wadi trail to the Great Place. Nakhtsobek, if you can check the worker's village and talk to your men on the mountain trail, we can meet you on the other side and figure out what to do next."

"Yes," Nakhtsobek said. "Don't worry, we'll box them in, but we'll have to run. They've got a good lead on us."

Bai had used their distraction to slowly crawl backwards through the mud to his knife. Rolling over to hide his movement, he picked up the knife and staggered to his feet like a drunk. Then he turned quickly and raced toward Nakhtsobek's back with his knife raised.

Bai stopped suddenly with Nebamun's thrown dagger lodged in his neck.

Nakhtsobek reacted by turning in a crouch, but Bai was already on his back in the mud, his sightless eyes staring into eternity.

Setau sighed and rolled his eyes. "Well, I knew that would happen eventually. I'm surprised he lived *this* long."

#

The slow climb up the tight ventilation shaft from Pharaoh Setnakhte's dark tomb to the glaring light of the desert plateau made Ray feel as if he were being born again, blind and anxious as he fought his way up the rough limestone that snagged on his cloak and tore at the skin of his hands, elbows, and knees. In the deathly silence of the shaft, Ray heard the breathing and sandy scrapings of Itennu above him and Bull behind. Startled rats squeaked and scuttled away. Beetles crunched under his arms and legs, although he was more concerned about the scorpions he must be crawling over in the darkness. When they finally reached the surface, they all lay on their backs on the warm stone, panting and blinking at the turquoise blue sky, lost in their own thoughts.

Now, the three of them stood atop the towering cliffs on the western rim of the Great Place; the dividing line between the sacred valleys where historic kings dreamed of eternity in their deep rock tombs and the hostile plain of salty limestone at their backs that marked the edge of the great Western Desert. The afternoon breeze in their faces carried a hint of damp soil from the fields by the silver Nile and the distant sounds of the busy city on the east bank, where the golden tips of temple flagpoles glittered in the sunlight above colorful linen pennants. On the closer west bank, the mortuary temples of the pharaohs mixed with walled administrative complexes of warehouses, work-places, and living spaces where priests and scribes managed the vast holdings of the gods or sold funeral goods and services to the bereaved. Thebes was a microcosm of the empire: mud-brick dwellings mixed with sprawling monumental structures that an-chored human lives and aspirations to the whims and desires of the gods. As Ray gazed out over the cities of the living and the dead spread out below, separated only by a brief river crossing like the fragile dividing line between life and death, he felt as if this might be the last time he'd ever see this eternal city.

\#

What do they say every day in their hearts,
those who are far from Thebes?
They spend their day blinking at its name,
if only we had it, they say—
The bread there is tastier than cakes made with goose fat,
its water is sweeter than honey,
one drinks of it till one gets drunk.
Oh! That is how one lives at Thebes.

\#

Of course, this same eternal city was the one where Ray's father had been wrongly executed, and this was an act that he could never forgive. He still didn't understand why it had happened, or why the gods had allowed such an injustice to occur, but Hapu had been destroyed by the same administrative system he had supported his entire life. Was this how his own life would end? Lies had won over truth, the oracle of Ptah had been fooled, and maat was out of balance. Could he really do anything about it, or was his goal to protect Bull doomed to end in failure because the gods had turned against them? Were they headed to safety in Pi-Ramesses, or were they just walking into a trap set by patient enemies?

"We're free," Itennu said.

Ray blinked, startled out of his thoughts. "What?"

"We escaped. Nobody escapes from the House of Death. And we got past the Medjay. We're free."

Ray turned and looked at the sandy desolation of the plateau and the wavering indistinct shapes of mirages over the glaring desert horizon. "Free. That's one way to look at it."

Ray knew he should feel more enthusiasm, but he kept thinking about his father and the long journey ahead of them with few supplies. He guessed that they were about three days away from Abydos over rough terrain and rarely used trails. They would be able to find water, but he wasn't as sure about finding food along the way. If they reached Abydos, a boat could take them the rest of the way to Pi-Ramesses.

Bull just stared at the view of Thebes and brushed sand off his arms.

With a final glance at the necropolis far below, Ray pulled the hood of his cloak over his head and started walking north. "It's almost sunset. Let's go before the spirits start rising from their tombs for the evening. We've got a long walk ahead of us."

#

Tentopet felt exhausted. Paniwi had worked her relentlessly for almost a month. When they weren't getting paid to dance, the entire troupe rehearsed every morning, took a break to sleep during the heat of the afternoon, and continued their exercises in the evening. Although Tentopet felt stronger than she ever had in her life, she had also lost weight despite eating more food. This evening, she and Paniwi were performing at a large retirement party for the sixty-year-old General Imhotep, a famous man from a long line of nobles who had served many pharaohs. Still calling herself Tyti, she had performed acrobatic and humorous dances for two hours with only short breaks before Paniwi signaled that they could stop. The musicians playing the harp, oboe, and sistra smiled and grabbed jars of beer. Tentopet and Paniwi wiped down their sweaty bodies with towels before tying filmy striped sashes around their waists.

There were about thirty military men from the Pharaoh Division in the courtyard along with a few wives dressed in their nicest linen sheath dresses, beaded necklaces, and gold or silver armbands. Servants worked their way through the crowd refilling beer jars and wine cups. Bowls of food had been set out earlier on low tables but were now picked over, leaving little for the performers to snack on. Braziers and oil lamps burned around the courtyard and the small pond circled by shadowy trees in the garden. The old general sat on an ebony wood chair that looked similar to a throne with ivory inlays and an image of Horus on the back made out of precious stones and silver, and everyone knew this to be a recent gift from Pharaoh Ramesses, the living god. While keeping his eyes on Tentopet, now poking through the food bowls looking for something to eat, Imhotep slowly got to his feet using a heavy walking stick and hobbled over to stand beside her. He held a cup of wine in his free hand.

"I can have the servants bring more food if you like," Imhotep said. "You've worked hard tonight. I wouldn't want you to go hungry. And I'm sure you need wine."

Tentopet smiled at the general and offered a slight bow as he handed her the cup of wine. "Thank you, General."

"You are a beautiful and accomplished dancer. I saw you perform once before here in Abydos, which is why I contacted Paniwi and asked that you dance for me tonight."

"I'm flattered, General. We appreciate your generous support." She hoped he wasn't going to ask her for some kind of private performance after the party. It seemed unlikely with his broken leg, and most clients knew better than to ask in the first place, but she knew her dancing could get the men overexcited.

The musicians who accompanied the dancers to their shows were also their bodyguards when necessary, but they were in a room full of army officers and she hoped there wouldn't be any trouble.

Imhotep lowered his voice and moved a little closer. Nobody else was near enough to hear them as the noisy party continued, so she started to worry. "There is more you should know. I have watched you grow, princess, and I'm impressed with what you have accomplished. You were very wise to get away from that nest of vipers in the royal court."

Tentopet stopped breathing and her eyes widened. The fig she had picked up squirted juice through her fingers as she involuntarily tensed her hand. She couldn't believe that someone had recognized her.

"Ah," said Imhotep, placing his hand on her shoulder. "I see I've upset you. Don't worry."

She took a hesitant breath, still afraid to look at him, wondering what she would have to do so that he would keep her secret. She felt as if she were falling into a black pit of despair.

"I will keep your secret. And I want you to know that you can come to me in Thebes at any time for help. Many of us have been harmed or threatened by Queen Teya and her friends, and we have few strategies available to us when a hostile queen decides we are threats or inconveniences. Both pharaohs come to me for advice on military and administrative matters, and Queen Teya has never liked the relationship I have with them. Unfortunately, I have had to scatter my own children in temples and administrative posts all over the empire to keep them safe, when they really should have had the benefits of regular attendance at the royal court. As for myself, the only tactical move I can make now is to retire to my estate in Thebes as Pharaoh has asked. The farmlands and servants that the pharaohs have given me as rewards, along with the lands that were awarded to my ancestors, allow me to live well and maintain our family's power as nobles, and as I get older I no longer feel the need to visit that nest of vipers in Pi-Ramesses."

Tentopet breathed a sigh of relief and felt the tension flow out of her body. She leaned against a wall for support. "You're the only person who has recognized me since I left the golden house."

"I understand," said Imhotep, offering her a stool as he sat on another beside it. "Forgive me; I need to sit to rest my leg."

Tentopet settled onto the stool and quickly emptied her cup. Imhotep caught the eye of a servant and signaled for them to bring more wine. "You should try the honey cakes or the marsh mallow. They're both excellent."

"So you're not asking anything of me, General?"

Imhotep gave her a kindly smile. "Certainly not. I merely wish to help you. And I mean it when I say you can come to me for help at any time. I may be retired, but I still have connections and wealth if you need it. And I can protect you if you need a place to hide. Does your great father or mother know where you are?"

Tentopet shook her head, and thoughts of them made her sad. "They do not. I had to leave suddenly, and it's better if nobody knows where I am."

"Yes, I understand. I assume that's why you became a dancer with Paniwi."

"It's one of the few skills I have. I can read and write, but I can't take a scribe's job because it would draw too much attention."

"I can always help you find work if you need it."

"I appreciate that, General. It actually feels good to talk to someone about this. I always feel that I have to be careful about what I say. I like working for Paniwi, and I've learned much more about the world than I did living in the cage of the golden house, but it's good to know I have a friend."

"Indeed. You're a smart young woman. I would expect nothing less from your family."

Tentopet thought for a moment about Imhotep's offer and the opportunities it might eventually open up. "General, I've decided that I will visit you in Thebes. But it will be quite some time before I feel safe doing so. I've had problems there, and I worry about being recognized, or even worse things than that. I'm sure you understand."

"My offer will stand. I also have good connections there with the vizier and many others in the local government, so I can make problems go away when necessary."

Tentopet felt as if the gods were on her side now. Perhaps they appreciated all that she had accomplished on her own, and the obstacles she had overcome, since she left the golden house.

They both spotted the smiling Paniwi coming toward them through the crowd, and Tentopet noted the eyes of many men watching her cross the room. Her skin still glistened from her dancing. Just before she arrived, Tentopet rested her hand on Imhotep's arm and smiled at him. "General, I have a favor to ask. If you hear any news of the royal friend, Ray, his father Hapu, or Prince Ramesses, please find a way to let me know. I've heard that they're missing."

Imhotep covered her hand with his own and replied in a whisper. "Of course, princess. Of course."

#

Ray blinked as something poked him in the back, then squinted since he was facing the rising sun. "Bull? What is it?"

No answer. It wasn't Bull.

Ray heard the shuffling of men and animals, as if an army were moving past nearby. As he became more alert, he realized something wasn't right about his body other than his sore muscles. A gravelly voice spoke as he was prodded again.

"Get up!"

Ray gasped when he realized that his wrists were tied together. He remembered only how tired they all were when they had stopped for the night just outside of Abydos. Low on water and stretching their food, sleep was the only thing that could keep them going long enough to reach the city. The cooler hours of darkness were the best time for them to travel, and they had intended to stop only for a brief rest, but they had all gone to sleep immediately. Ray still wasn't awake enough to understand who was talking or why his wrists were tied, but he sat up and looked around.

A fat man in dusty and ragged clothes, incongruously decorated with an impressive gold collar around his neck and many gold armbands, gave Ray a smile composed of four teeth. "Up!"

A second man behind Ray hauled him straight up to his feet as if he weighed nothing.

"What's going on? Who are you?" Ray stammered.

The fat man slapped his chest, which raised a cloud of dust from the striped cloth of his long garment. "You may call me Master Hemesh! I own you now!"

"What?"

Hemesh yelled into Ray's ear, making him flinch. "Are you deaf?"

"No!" Ray yelled back into Hemesh's face. Then something thumped the back of his head, giving him an instant headache. "You can't own me! I'm a free man!"

"You *were* a free man. Now I own you. At least until I sell you to the Royal Butler Ramessesemperre. He oversees the copper mines at Timna. I get more for strong men and skilled women, and you look kind of spindly, but your friends should bring a decent price—at least four *deben* each. Maybe six for the big one."

"You can't just make slaves out of us!"

"Ha! I have a papyrus from Vizier To that says I can make a slave out of anybody I want to sell to the royal mines, except for nobles. I have a quota to meet before we reach the boat in Abydos, and you just made it for me. Thebes came up short on heads this trip, even though I pay the police chief and the mayor to collect criminals for the mines. And I can't depend on the police chief in Abydos—they never hold their criminals for long."

Ray started to say something until he noticed the long line of supply donkeys and shambling men with their wrists tied. Many of them had beards, even though they appeared to be Egyptian. A long cloud of dust hung in the air where they walked, tired and silent, their lifeless eyes focused on the ground. Some of them wore bandages wrapped around their heads like mummies to cover the wounds from having their noses and ears cut off for their crimes.

"Where are my friends?"

Hemesh pointed behind Ray. He turned to see a red-faced Itennu kneeling in the sand while he rubbed his sore head with his tied hands. A slaver stood behind him holding a short club. Bull stood quietly nearby with his wrists tied and his hood over his head, looking puzzled by all the activity. Ray sighed, thinking at least Bull was safe for the moment, even though they might all end up dying in the dreaded copper mines, which he knew to be a one-way trip. The Great Prison of Thebes would have been a better fate. Their only choice seemed to be to go with the slavers until they found an opportunity to escape.

The gods had certainly abandoned them now.

#

Nestled among the neatly arranged mansions of the wealthy where the Nile flowed past the western side of Pi-Ramesses, the home of Chief General Hori was hosting an unusual late-night dinner. When Hori was in residence, his house was known to be a lively place for social events among the otherwise quiet grid of stately homes in his wealthy neighborhood, but his immediate neighbors had learned it was better not to bother him with any complaints about his parties.

Along the back of the main house, a pillared porch faced a formal garden courtyard decorated with twelve sycamore fig trees forming a neat rectangle around a large pool. Oil lamps hung from the tree limbs cast bright reflections on the pool, rippling whenever Queen Teya slowly swam through the water. From his large chair, where the carved heads and paws of lions formed the arm rests and legs, Chief General Hori watched her sleek form gliding through the water, and Pentawere knew he was thinking what many of her male admirers would think and never say when they were in her presence. This awareness of the Hori's crude thoughts annoyed him, but he also knew that this was one of the ways that his mother controlled her minions in the golden house.

Pantry Chief Paibakamana and Court Butler Mastesuria were busy clearing empty food bowls from the various low tables and pouring more wine while only sneaking glances at the queen. They knew it could be dangerous for them to do otherwise, so they pretended to focus on their work. Normally confined to the golden house and its grounds, Teya had requested that Paibaka-mana and Mastesuria attend to assist with the dinner, although Pentawere wasn't sure why when the general's servants would have been sufficient to handle the elaborate meal.

Pentawere mostly ignored the priest, which was probably what the priest wanted as he ignored the queen and stared off into the distance as if he were inspired to think deep thoughts. Merubaste—Lector Priest and Assistant to the High Priest Bak-enkhons of the Temple of Amun-Re—liked to quietly lurk in the background when important meetings were going on. Pentawere knew he was one of those people who pretended to remain aloof but was listening for anything he might be able to use to the advantage of himself or his powerful temple.

When Teya stood up in the shallow pool and turned to face them, one of Hori's attractive female servants tried to hand her a towel, but she ignored it and locked her gaze on the general. The dark water rippled around her thighs. "All right, Hori. I have eaten your food and cooled off in your pool. You may give us your news."

Hori's voice always sounded like a rumbling from deep inside a mountain. "Yes, my Queen. We have a report from Standard-Bearer Didu, but you're not going to like all of it. His investigation has taken him to Thebes. The Royal Tutor Hapu is no longer a problem. He was executed by the Medjay for participating in a tomb robbery."

Teya gasped in surprise, then clapped her hands with delight. "Excellent! But tomb robbery? Who would believe that?"

"We don't have all the details, but our people managed to get a confession out of a real tomb robber. He named Hapu in return for a lighter sentence."

Paibakamana and Mastesuria started to leave with stacks of empty food bowls, but Pentawere gestured for them to stand and wait.

"And how was he executed?" Teya accepted the towel from the servant and started drying herself.

"On the wood."

"Hmm. Painful, but an excellent choice. I never liked that man. He thought he knew everything, and Sesi trusted him far too much with the children. Why didn't Meryey's assassins get to him first?"

"They tried, Majesty, but there was some confusion. We thought the assassins would reach them before our investigator did, but it didn't work out that way. Meryey's men have all been killed, except for one who is in the custody of the Medjay in Thebes."

Teya shook her head and stepped out of the pool, dropping

her towel on the stone paving. Standing by the table, she poured herself a cup of wine, drank it quickly, then poured another. Pentawere watched her jaw muscles working as she clenched and unclenched her teeth. "This is bad. What are you going to do about it?"

"I have already issued the order for him to be executed. Until then, he will remain isolated."

Teya finished her cup of wine and poured another before glaring at the general. "You will remember your place and stand when speaking to me."

Startled, Hori stood up. Pentawere smiled as he watched the solid and imposing figure looking uncomfortable for a change, keeping his eyes lowered to show respect. In the flickering light from the braziers and the lamps, the scars on his muscular chest and shoulders appeared to dance like angry snakes. His pristine white kilt, belted with gold cords, looked unusually formal and correct for a military man. A broad gold collar, the Gold of Valor presented to him by the living god, gleamed in the light.

Teya took two steps closer to Hori, glaring straight into his eyes. "Now, what about the prince and his friend?"

"They have eluded our investigator for now, but he continues to search. The Medjay in Thebes are helping him."

"You're telling me that two boys, one of whom is the Hawk-in-the-Nest, have escaped all of your attempts to hunt them down. And that Meryey's assassins also failed."

Hori shrugged. "Well, the assassins are foreigners, Majesty. They don't have the same level of training and experience that we do."

"And they show their ignorance by worshipping the wrong gods," Merubaste added.

Pentawere set down his wine cup and watched carefully. He could read his mother well enough that he knew something interesting was about to happen.

"And you used foreigners because...."

"We couldn't expect Egyptian soldiers to kill one of our own princes, Majesty. And we needed the greatest secrecy to protect all of our lives."

Teya threw the wine from her cup into Hori's face. He blinked the wine out of his eyes, but otherwise did not flinch. "As long as the prince is alive and free, he is a threat, and so is his friend. My son will not sit on the throne as long as the prince is alive. Do you understand?"

"Yes, Majesty. I understand."

"Now, your investigator, this Didu. Why did you pick him for this task?"

Hori licked his dry lips. "I did not select him, Highness. The living god Pharaoh Ramesses chose Didu for this task. Didu believes he is to capture the prince and his friend and return them here."

Teya poured another cup of wine and threw that one in his face as well. "That can't happen. You know that, right? Their return would be far worse for us than anything you can imagine. To be specific, their return would be very bad for you, because you will be revealed as the traitor when Sesi starts asking questions."

"Majesty, we have Pasai for that purpose. We're still holding him in isolation."

Teya gave him an evil smile. "If the prince returns to Pi-Ramesses, I can assure you that you will hang from the city walls by your heels unless you choose to slit your own throat first. Is that clear?"

Paibakamana and Mastesuria stood rooted to the spot, still holding the empty bowls and casting worried looks at each other. Merubaste covered his mouth to hide a smile.

Pentawere cleared his throat. "Mother, perhaps it's time for a change. Now that I've been named Commander in Chief of Elite Foot Troops, I can oversee this investigation to make sure we get the results we want. It appears that the general is out of his depth."

Hori glanced at Pentawere. Teya drank another cup of wine. "That's an excellent idea, my brilliant son." She looked at Hori. "Do you see any problem with that, General Hori?"

Hori hesitated and took a deep breath. He kept his eyes lowered, but Pentawere could see that the general was still looking at her body. "That is not a problem, Highness. I am the dust on your feet and will do whatever you require, as always."

"You may kiss my feet."

Pentawere was enjoying himself as the great warrior hesitated again, then lowered his entire body to the ground to lie prostrate and cautiously kiss her feet, probably thinking she would kick him in the face.

Sensing danger, Merubaste spoke up. "Would you like me to kiss your feet as well, Highness?"

"You may not, Priest. That reward is not for you, and you know enough to stay in your place. In fact, I had almost forgotten you were here. Where is your master?"

"Bakenkhons is in Thebes, Highness. I am certain that he regrets his absence from this meeting."

Teya ignored him and searched for more wine. Finding none, she pinned her two servants with the force of her gaze. Startled, Mastesuria dropped a clay bowl and it shattered on the stone pavers, but he didn't move. "The two of you will maintain your silence about everything you've heard here, or you will find yourselves dismembered in an unmarked grave in the desert. Do you understand?"

The two servants nodded and said, "Yes, Majesty. Of course, Majesty."

"You will continue with your other kitchen tasks as I have directed. Your reports will now go to Pentawere, and I will communicate with you through him. Now, get me more wine!"

Six

1184 BCE—Royal Mines of Timna

Year 4 of His Majesty, King of Upper and Lower Egypt, Chosen by Re, Beloved of Amun, Pharaoh Setnakhte, Third Month of Akhet (Season of Inundation), Day 26

#

The first week of slogging through the desert had been the worst. The moisture in the air close to the Nile had vanished as soon as they were a day away from the river, and it seemed as if the towering spikes of the steep mountain ranges on either side of the broad wash were there to focus the heat on them. They had enough water in the clay jugs and water skins, refilled whenever they came across the wells dug by the armies and laborers of previous pharaohs to support this major east-west trade route, but food was carefully rationed. Supplies were carried on donkeys—one per man—and each captive trudged along the dry riverbed beside his donkey, but heat and hunger became Ray's constant companions for this journey. The rocky ground was relatively flat, but the glare was bright and Ray wished he had access to kohl to paint around his eyes. Without it, his face was always tired from the squinting he had to do to protect his vision.

With no place to go if they tried to run away, they were allowed to move forward or behind along the long line to talk to others, but it felt like a lot of extra work to expend the energy. That was why a week went by before Ray found himself talking to the man whose face was wrapped like a mummy in the line just ahead of him. Thinking he would pass the time with the man and avoid thinking about his own discomfort, Ray was startled to learn that he knew this person whose nose and ears had been cut off in Thebes. He was Neferabu, the artist whose work he had admired at the Festival of Drunkenness outside the house of High Priest Bakenkhons. Neferabu didn't like to talk much because the bandages scraped across the crusty wounds where his nose and ears used to be whenever he moved his mouth. Over the course of several days, Neferabu told him his story since he they had last seen each other. Neferabu had apparently been talked into robbing a tomb in the Great Place with his friend and a small boy. Ray learned a few days later that the small boy was Ruta, who had helped Ray and Bull find food at the funeral where Itennu had been working. He also explained that his original punishment had been reduced after he was forced to lie about the involvement of another man, but he wouldn't reveal the man's identity, and didn't think it really mattered now that the man was dead. This had created a sense of guilt in Neferabu that was stronger than the pain he felt from his head wounds, and he believed the great god Ptah was sending him to the mines to continue his punishment and that it was the right thing to do. Ray said whatever he could think of to calm Neferabu's torment, but it didn't seem to help. Ray knew it was time to drop back into his assigned place in line whenever Neferabu fell into silence, and that bothered him because he couldn't really do anything to help the man.

Bull was in the line behind Ray, walking along as if he were unaffected by their new ordeal. He always looked as if he were out for a morning stroll along the Nile. Ray checked on him throughout the day, but he remained happy and unconcerned. Ray envied him. Although Ray was distracting himself through his conversations, despair lurked in the back of his mind, and he knew he had to keep pushing it back so it wouldn't come to dominate his thoughts. Things didn't look good, but he wasn't ready to give up. As long as he was still alive, there was a chance things could get better.

Farther back, Itennu trudged along with his hood over his head. They were all still wearing the sem-priest robes that Itennu had stolen for them, and Ray was glad to have his because of the extra protection from the sun that the long garment offered. Although the pleated robes held some of the sweat and steam coming off his body, the dirty white linen dried fast and kept him more comfortable than he'd be without it. Itennu hadn't said much the first few days, except for the occasional comment about Amun-Re teaching him a new lesson. However, Itennu couldn't figure out what he was meant to learn. He continued to meditate on this question throughout each day, briefly summarizing his thoughts on the matter when Ray stopped by for a visit. Ray didn't understand why Itennu thought all their problems were being created by the god, rather than through their own bad decisions, but he didn't want to argue with the young priest. If Itennu wanted to believe that the god was training him for something greater in his life, Ray wasn't going to try and dissuade him, especially if his belief would help get him through each day.

Ray didn't know how many captives were in the line, or how many guards were escorting them, but he saw they had to split up into multiple cedar boats for their crossing of the Eastern Sea. They had seen water birds when they were about a day away from it, and Ray had been surprised that they were approaching a large body of water. He had heard of the Eastern Sea, but assumed it would have been much more distant. Although he had lost count of the days and the terrain mostly looked the same for the entire trip, he knew they had been walking for at least a week. A small trading settlement along the water also held an organized little harbor where trading ships were moored along the banks beside an Egyptian warship. Itennu had told him that this was Egypt's main trading route to the east, and they had watched two small caravans passing them in the opposite direction along the way. The settlement was also protected by a small Egyptian fortress with high mud-brick walls. The place was busier than Ray had expected, with dozens of men and a few women going about their business, interspersed with groups of donkeys all over the place. He saw some unusual clothing, but was able to identify groups of the nomadic Bedouin and Canaanites who ran huge teams of donkeys along the trade routes, along with a few Meshwesh, Hittites, Philistines, and traders from the land of Punt.

Several boats were needed to move the entire group across the sea, and they sagged into the shade of a palm tree cluster as Master Hemesh haggled with captains at the docks. As their group crowded in under the relatively small amount of shade, the long line of captives continued to arrive and jostling began as their guards bunched them all together. During this distraction, Ray watched a short man with bandages wrapped around his head crawl away under a line of tied donkeys. When the man stood up to run, one of the guards jogged a few steps and then hurled a hunting lasso—a long rope with stones tied to the ends. The spinning lasso whipped through the air and wrapped itself around the running man's legs, knocking him down on his face. The guard then casually walked over to the fallen man and picked him up.

Ray had gone to sleep on the floor of his boat as soon as their group was loaded with the donkeys. The floor smelled like fish. Additional supplies had been purchased at the settlement and loaded along with them. The donkeys were watered and fed well, as they had been throughout the trip, and additional loaves of bread were given to each of the captives. The last thing Ray remembered after getting on the boat was the taste of the fresh bread, and when he woke up he still had a chunk of it in his mouth. Hours later, the captives were herded off the boat and the long walk continued. Ray didn't care any more. It seemed as if their journey would never end.

After another exhausted sleep period, where Ray woke up every couple of hours to look at the bright field of stars in the sky and wonder if his father might be looking back at him, they ate their morning meal of bread and water and continued along a well-worn trail through the rocky hills. Without the boat ride, Ray wouldn't have been able to tell that they had gone anywhere because the stark terrain hadn't changed and this was just another dead place where vegetation refused to grow.

Later that morning, Ray felt a sense of relief when he saw they could be nearing their destination. Even though they might end up dying in the mines, at least this monotonous part of their journey would be over. They passed a few ruined stone dwellings along with piles of broken tools and pottery. Approaching from the east, he saw craggy vertical cliffs a thousand feet high that formed a half-circle around a flat mining area that might be forty miles across. Over the next couple of hours, they moved closer to the western cliffs and saw the remains of several former mining camps and small ruined temples along the way. Many of these former camps were near large ragged holes in the ground a short distance from ancient copper smelting furnaces, charcoal pits, and slag piles. The city of Pi-Ramesses had its own large smelters as part of its weapon production facilities, and even Ray knew enough to understand that it was much more sophisticated than what he was seeing here in Timna.

As they neared the cliffs in the middle of the valley, smelters and mine shafts began to appear with more frequency. The echoing sounds of rock crushing and hammering filled the air along with smoke from smelter fires. They followed a broad avenue through a more modern mining camp of stone and mud-brick buildings that could have housed a few thousand workers packed close together. Piles of slag, charcoal, and copper ore formed giant mounds near the smelters.

At their approach to the base of the cliffs, a man with graying shoulder-length hair and a short beard, wearing a striped kilt belted with leather, emerged from what appeared to be an administration building constructed of white stone slabs. As he got closer, Ray saw that he wore a black leather eyepatch over his left eye. His narrow face, with a nose like a hawk's beak, made him look like a predatory bird. Master Hemesh started toward the man as the long line of new recruits was herded into a tight group by their guards. The donkeys were separated from the men and walked over to a watering basin.

When Master Hemesh was about to speak, the man held up his hand for silence, stopping Hemesh in his tracks. The man studied the group of new recruits, his one eye studying each face as a cloud of dust from their passage caught up to them and drifted past. "I am Ramessesemperre—Royal Butler to the good god Pharaoh Ramesses III, may he live a long, prosperous, and healthy life! I am Overseer of the Pharaoh's Copper Mines of the Timna Valley. If you speak to me, you may call me 'overseer' or 'lord' if you want to avoid harm."

Ramessesemperre raised his arms and gestured at the mining operation around them. "This is your new home! Most of you will live here until you die, which may happen sooner than later, but you will be treated well if you follow the rules. Rule breakers will not be treated well. You will work alongside other Egyptians, but you will also be working with men from many other distant lands, and I expect all of you to treat each other with respect. When there is an accident, your life may depend on help from the man working beside you. There is no escape from Timna, so you might as well get used to it. You will have the freedom of the mining camp when you're not working, and you will find many of the businesses and temples here that you knew from your former homes. You will be paid with food and a place to live, but you may also find opportunities to earn more so that you can trade for services or make offerings at your favorite temple. Hathor is our patron goddess of mining, and her temple is very popular. We have a beer house, a brothel, funeral services, and other businesses to make you feel at home."

Master Hemesh started to say something, but Ramessesemperre held up his hand for silence once again. "Now, you may have heard stories about how dangerous it is to work in the mines, or how men age quickly doing this kind of labor, or how half of each new workforce is killed within their first year—and it's all true! However, you will also find that this kind of work focuses the mind. You will learn new skills and you will learn much about yourself. You can make a good life for yourself here—because you don't have any choice—or your life can be short and brutal. The choice is yours! I hope you make the right choice."

Water skins were being passed around the group, which Ray now estimated to be about three hundred people. Bull and Itennu had moved up beside Ray. Master Hemesh was now speaking to Ramessesemperre, who continued to study the men rather than looking at the slave master. When Hemesh was done speaking, Ramessesemperre held up three fingers. Hemesh shook his head and held up six fingers. Still without looking at Hemesh, the overseer raised five fingers, and he seemed pleased when Hemesh sighed, nodded, and walked away. The negotiation was over.

Ray took a loaf of fresh bread from one of the bowls being passed around. When he bit into it, the flavor filled his mouth with delight. He felt a cautious hint of optimism about his new situation.

As the overseer continued to watch, guards herded them toward long rows of empty dwellings and told them to rest. Tomorrow, they would be introduced to their new jobs deep beneath the earth. Ray, Bull, and Itennu stepped into the cooler darkness of a small dwelling that could sleep four people in moderate comfort on the stone benches. Four feather pillows were stacked on a low table in a corner. Neferabu entered behind them and curled up on a bench, hiding his face and speaking to no one.

They were now residents of Timna—the gateway to the afterlife.

#

When Khait returned to Pi-Ramesses after her one month of service to Hathor, she felt like a different person and she was anxious to tell her father about it. As soon as she stepped from the boat where she had spent the last ten days, she made her way past the mansions of the wealthy to the golden house, knowing that her father would be in his small office doing his job as the Overseer of Cattle. Panhayboni had told her many times that his important position entitled him to work in the ring of outer administrative offices outside of Pharaoh's court, and that it was an excellent stepping stone to the most exalted jobs working directly with Pharaoh. After checking in with Panouk, the Overseer of the Harem, Khait took one of the private interior hallways that connected the harem with the administrative wing right next to Panhayboni's office. If she had gone in from the public entrance at the opposite end of the building, the guard would have escorted her to her father's office and announced her, spoiling the surprise.

If she had timed it right, Khait figured they could have lunch together so she could tell her father all about her trip to Thebes. Panouk had informed her that Pharaoh Ramesses, Queen Isis, Prince Pentawere, and invited courtiers were in Thebes for the burial of Prince Amanakhopshaf, so there were fewer people around than usual. Seeing no one in the administrative corridor, Khait quietly stepped over to the partially open office door. Hearing voices, she hesitated and peered inside, not wanting to disturb an important meeting.

"I told you we would not be having direct contact again, Kitchen Boy," said Queen Teya, "but your failure to do your job correctly has forced this meeting."

"Majesty, Mastesuria and I have been adding the powder to his food twice a day as you requested."

"Then how do you explain his health? Why is he still alive?" Teya asked.

"Pharaoh is very strong," Panhayboni said. "His divine connection to the god gives him healing powers that mortal men do not have. We just have to wait."

Teya snorted. "You can wait all you want, Overseer of Cattle. I want results. Sesi and most of his court are in Thebes right now, and I don't want to waste this opportunity."

"We don't want to make it obvious that the living god has been poisoned," Panhayboni said. "We must be patient to avoid suspicion."

"Patience is a virtue," said the priest Merubaste. "The gods reward us for it, especially when we're trying to send a pharaoh to meet Osiris."

Khait couldn't believe what she was hearing. Were they

actually trying to poison Pharaoh Setnakhte? Was that even possible? Feeling a little dizzy, she leaned against the wall.

"Kitchen Boy, I want you to add more powder to his food. For all three of his daily meals. Everyone knows he's been sick for a while now, so I don't think a little extra push to move things along will raise any suspicions."

"As you wish, Majesty," Paibakamana said. "I will do as you command."

"Yes, and if you do, I will reward you. If you fail, your life will be short and painful."

Khait shook her head. Maybe they were just using his father's office and he wasn't an active participant in their plan. She peered around the doorway again to see if anyone else was in the office.

Panhayboni cleared his throat. "Let me know if you need more of the powder."

"The temple also has its sources," noted Merubaste. "We will help however we can."

Khait gasped and jerked her head back from the doorway.

"Did you hear something?" Teya asked.

Khait sprinted into the private corridor and back to the harem, hoping that no one in the office had reacted quickly enough to check the corridor she was in. Spotting a few women bathing in one of the smaller pools of the harem courtyard, she slowed to a walk, slipped out of her dress, and joined them. When Panouk, the Overseer of the Harem, arrived a short time later, Khait was deep in conversation with the other women in the pool, trying not to think distressing thoughts about her father. Panouk frowned, studying the women in the pool. They continued to ignore him and he left by the private corridor.

Khait had no idea what to do with the information she had overheard, or whether it would be safe to mention it to anyone, but she felt that she ought to do something. She certainly couldn't discuss it with her father. She hadn't even been back in the golden house for a full day. She should have stayed in Thebes with Shepsit. And what if someone in her father's office had seen her running away? Would she even live through the night? But no, if they had seen her, they would have come for her by now. She closed her eyes and sank lower in the pool. She needed to calm down so she could think.

As far as Khait could tell, she was safe. For now.

Seven

1184 BCE—Royal Mines of Timna

Year 4 of His Majesty, King of Upper and Lower Egypt, Chosen by Re, Beloved of Amun, Pharaoh Setnakhte, Fourth Month of Akhet (Season of Inundation), Day 17

#

Over a period of two weeks, Ray felt like he was turning into an underground creature that lived in darkness and burrowed through stone, something like an ant or a rat. He spent most of his time on his back or his stomach with his arms stretched ahead of him to wield his hammer and bronze chisel, his hoe, or a pick with a short wooden handle. Each horizontal tunnel was about three feet wide when it was finished, but it was tighter at the front end where Ray was chopping. When he filled a leather basket full of debris or copper ore in the light of his oil lamp, he would signal by tugging on the rope and the basket would be dragged away beneath him as he lifted his body. Occasional vertical shafts in the roof behind him allowed air and light into the tunnel. Ray was only thirty feet below the surface in this tunnel, but some were as deep as one hundred and twenty feet with several horizontal galleries branching off the vertical entry shaft. When the miners went to work, they used a rope along with hand and foot holds to climb down into the dry tunnels where they could trace the veins of copper ore through the soft sandstone and limestone. In areas where the veins of ore widened into large deposits, the horizontal shafts were widened into larger chambers supported by pillars of stone that the miners left in place.

It was in one of these larger chambers that Ray thought he was going to die.

Under normal circumstances, it took ten workers to create a single mine shaft. On this day, Ray's arm muscles were burning because he had spent most of the morning as the prospector digging in the most restricted space to follow the vein of ore at the front of the shaft. Behind him, Bull and Neferabu widened the shaft further and took the debris to the vertical shaft, where Itennu and another man on the surface hauled the baskets to the surface. Others sorted the copper ore and dumped the debris while a scribe documented the quantity of ore they were hauling out of the earth. They took periodic breaks to drink water or beer and eat bread. With all the exercise and food, Ray found he was slowly growing more muscular, but the work was still exhausting and he could barely lift his arms at the end of each day. On a few days, he had also had breathing problems from the tunnel dust. The mine physician knew the same remedies to help him breathe as his physician back in Pi-Ramesses, but he also had some new tricks that worked faster, and Ray was impressed by his healing magic.

After their most recent break, Bull had wriggled into the

lead position where he was always the fastest miner despite the tight space. He had quickly created a chamber at the end that was large enough for Neferabu to work beside him, and was now becoming wide enough for Ray to join them as well. They had just loaded their baskets with copper ore when Ray heard the terrifying sound of thundering rock and dirt pouring into the small chamber.

Bull and Itennu dove to one side and Ray lunged out of the chamber back into their new tunnel. He scrabbled backwards hoping to get clear and make enough room for Bull and Neferabu to escape, trying to take only small sips of the dusty air as he lurched through the sudden darkness. When he reached the first vertical air shaft, he saw that much of the dust was being drawn up the shaft toward the light, but continued on until he was well out of the roiling cloud and the thunder began to settle. Emerging into the vertical exit shaft, he yelled for help. As the two silhouetted men at the top of the shaft started climbing down, Ray watched for Bull or Neferabu to appear. Seeing nothing, he grabbed another oil lamp, took a few deep breaths, and crawled back into the tunnel to look for them.

Most of the way back to the chamber where the cave-in had occurred, Ray found an injured Neferabu gasping for air. Ray grabbed his wrists and started backing out of the tunnel again, wedging his body every few feet to drag Neferabu along. In his panic, he kept thinking of Bull and that got him moving faster. When he pulled Neferabu into the vertical exit shaft, the other two men took over. Ray bent over to inhale several deep breaths and scrambled back into the shaft again.

Barely aware that his hands, arms, and knees were slick with his own blood, Ray could think only of getting back to the chamber. When he reached it, he saw rock and dirt blocking the entrance. One of the picks lay nearby, so he grabbed it and frantically tore at the rocky barrier. He refused to believe that Bull's life, or his life, would end here beneath the earth in a place that was closer to the underworld than people would normally go. He imagined the great god Osiris listening to Ray's pick gouging chunks out of the rock pile in the tunnel far above his underworld throne.

Ray would not let Bull die. Not now. Not after their long journey, the hiding, the fighting, and all the other things they had done to keep the prince safe.

The pile of rocks blocking the chamber collapsed to one side as a hole opened up. Ray held up his oil lamp and saw what looked like the ghost of Bull on the other side before realizing that he was only covered in dust. Bull was using a leather basket and a hoe to drag debris away from the opening on his side, and he smiled when he saw Ray.

They used the ropes and the handholds in the vertical shaft to climb into the light where humans belonged. Neferabu lay on the ground with his eyes closed, but Ray could see that he was breathing. Itennu held Neferabu's hand and spoke to him in a calming voice. Neferabu's bandage had come off his head while Ray was dragging him through the tunnel, revealing the gaping red hole where his nose would have been before it was cut off. His ears were missing. Ray looked away as the mine physician ran up to them and dropped to his knees beside Neferabu. Someone handed Ray and Bull jars of beer, and Ray gradually became aware that a crowd of men stood around them. The scribe pointed at Ray and announced that he had saved the other men. The crowd cheered. Ray and his friends had survived what all of the miners feared.

Ramessesemperre pushed his way through the growing crowd and looked down at Neferabu as he demanded to know what had happened. Ray tried to order his thoughts and make the best explanation that he could, but he suddenly felt dizzy and weak and he was forced to sit down hard on the ground. He smelled and tasted dust and sweat. He noticed he was bleeding all over, but he didn't notice any pain. Ramessesemperre appeared to be saying something to him, but Ray couldn't hear any words. The sky was a brilliant blue.

Ray didn't remember anything after that.

#

Two weeks after her return to Pi-Ramesses, Khait doubted her memory. Despite what she thought she had heard in her father's office, it didn't seem possible that they were trying to poison Pharaoh Setnakhte, and nothing had happened since then. Three days after she had heard the plot, she braced herself and arranged to have dinner with her father, but everything seemed normal. She told Panhayboni of her experience with Shepsit and the Temple of Hathor, and how she was looking forward to going back so she could learn more and become a full priestess. Her father was delighted, pointing out how advantageous her new role would be in terms of her standing at court. She would have to continue with her weaving and dressmaking, of course, which carried its own benefits as a means to gather information and gossip from the queens as well as other important women of the court and the harem. These were all things that Panhayboni would normally say, and his casual manner put her at ease. Khait knew her father was a schemer whose main goal was to advance at court and become a wealthier man of influence, but she couldn't believe he would become involved in murder. Queen Teya held power over a lot of men, but if she was going to get their help to murder someone, Queen Isis would have been her first target since she was the Chief Royal Wife and therefore had more power than Teya, who was the Principal Royal Wife. Or was Teya's plan larger than that? Was she trying to remove the competition so that Pentawere would become the Hawk-in-the-Nest? Was she somehow involved in the murder of Prince Amanakhopshaf? Maybe if Panhayboni knew of a larger plan, he might support Queen Teya as a means to protect himself. If he did not support the queen, she might also consider him a threat and have him removed from court, or maybe even killed to keep her secret. But no, Khait refused to believe that her father would risk his life, and hers, to support the murder of a pharaoh.

Having satisfied herself that her father must be innocent, Khait started spending part of her time each day following Paibakamana. She wore a plain sheath dress, a simple wig, and modest face paint so that she wouldn't stand out so much among the servants. Paibakamana was easy enough to find since he was based in the kitchen with Mastesuria and many other servants. There were enough people bustling through the corridors near the kitchens that Khait was able to blend into the background to watch for Paibakamana, but she knew she had to be ready with an excuse as to why she was lurking in that area in case anyone should ask. With most of the staff, she could act superior and simply say she was on harem business, but some of the guards or the court officials might not be put off so easily. However, many of the people who might question her were still in Thebes for the funeral, or perhaps on their way back to Pi-Ramesses.

Early one morning, she saw little Pepi, the royal food taster, enter the kitchen. After a short time, Pepi left again and Khait followed Paibakamana and Mastesuria through the golden house as they carried bowls of food to Pharaoh Setnakhte's bedchamber. As they spoke to the guards outside the pharaoh's door, Khait used the distraction to hide in a nearby doorway out of their sight where she could still hear what they said. The guards admitted them, but she couldn't see what they were doing in the bedchamber, and it didn't sound like they said anything.

"Are you lost?" Pepi asked, appearing from nowhere and clearly aware that she wasn't lost.

Khait wasn't sure how to respond, and she knew she should have rehearsed something as she looked down at him. "I'm on harem business."

Pepi smirked and crossed his arms. "And what business would that be? Has the living god requested you?"

Khait hesitated again. "Yes. I was just waiting for the kitchen staff to leave."

"By hiding in this doorway?"

"I wasn't hiding. The pharaoh requested discretion."

"Interesting. We should report this to his physician since he hasn't spoken to anyone else for almost a month now."

Khait knew he was baiting her, but she wasn't sure what she could do about it without digging a deeper hole for herself. "Perhaps the messenger lied to me."

"And who was that?"

"Some servant. I don't recall. We have so many servants."

"This is true. But don't let me keep you from your appointment. If the living god managed to exert the effort to summon you, he must have something important to tell you."

"Oh, well, I just remembered I'll have to come back later. The messenger said I should come by this evening."

"I see. Well, I'll be here later when you return. And that will give me a chance to verify what you say, just to make sure there was no misinterpretation, of course. You know how servants can get messages wrong."

Khait wondered why Pepi wasn't causing more trouble, unless he planned to use this incident against her later on.

"I have to go," Khait said, quickly walking away and hoping she could catch up to the kitchen staff.

It was a long walk back to the kitchen, and Khait caught up with Paibakamana and Mastesuria while they were talking. Their reed sandals slapped heavily against the blue stone floors, covering any small noises she might make with her thin leather sandals while she moved closer.

"We have to use more. He's not dying fast enough, and Queen Teya will have our heads if he doesn't go soon," said Paibakamana.

"You mean she'll have *your* head. I just help you deliver the food."

Paibakamana snorted. "You know too much, my friend. If I go, you're going with me. She is not a forgiving queen."

"This is getting too dangerous. Maybe we should tell someone, like Queen Isis or someone else who's strong enough to protect us."

"Protection." Paibakamana sighed heavily. "You don't seem to understand. There is no protection. The queen is far too dangerous and she can make people disappear. Have you seen Princess Tentopet lately?"

"We heard she was training to be a priestess of Amun-Re in Thebes."

"That's what you're supposed to think. You live in the kitchen, so you don't know anything."

Paibakamana and Mastesuria stopped talking as three young male servants came around a corner and walked toward them. Khait's heart was beating fast and she hoped no one would pay attention to her, but she started looking for exits. As the servants passed them and continued on their way, Paibakamana glanced over his shoulder and saw Khait. He knew she was much too close.

Khait stopped as if she had forgotten something, then turned and walked in the opposite direction.

"My lady, where are you going?"

Khait ignored Paibakamana and continued walking. This was normal behavior since she was of higher status and didn't need to answer questions from servants. She was heading back toward the pharaoh's bedchamber, but knew she would reach other exits if she went far enough. Most of the rooms along this corridor belonged to members of the royal family, their body servants, and a few royal scribes who had to be available to the pharaoh at all times, but she couldn't very well hide in any of their rooms.

She heard heavy footsteps following her.

The male servants who had passed them a moment ago were gone now. Khait started moving faster, but she heard her followers speed up as well. Despite the pounding of her heart, Khait tried to maintain proper posture and keep herself from walking too fast. If they tried to stop her, she could always cause a commotion that would draw the guards and claim that the kitchen servants were chasing her. Which they were, of course.

Khait faltered and her eyes widened when she saw Queen Teya coming toward her with Pepi, Harem Overseer Panouk, and her father right behind her. Farther back, Chief General Hori and the priest Merubaste approached in deep conversation. They all spread out across the corridor when they saw her coming toward them. Something was definitely wrong. Pepi must have told the queen about her suspicious visit to the pharaoh's private area of the golden house. But how had Panhayboni been summoned so quickly? Had he been with the queen when Pepi arrived? What had Pepi told them? Had some big meeting been going on that also included Hori and Merubaste? She looked around, but there were no exits, and the kitchen servants were closing in behind her. Then she had to stop because she was surrounded and the queen moved up close to stare straight into her eyes. Khait tried to swallow, but her mouth had dried up. Her father avoided her gaze.

"Dressmaker! The little footstool tells me you came to see the living god Setnakhte."

"Why would I do that," Khait stammered, unable to think of anything else to say.

"Why indeed? Harem Overseer, repeat what you told Pepi."

Panouk looked like he was happy to be included. He put both hands flat on his large belly and stood a little straighter with a smug expression on his round face. "Pepi told me of his conversation with Khait, and I assured him that the young lady was not on any official business of the harem that I'm aware of, Your Highness. She is, of course, free to roam the golden house, but I would have been informed of any invitation from the living god Pharaoh Setnakhte—may he live and prosper in good health. So say I, Panouk, your most humble servant, Majesty."

"Pepi is mistaken," Khait said.

"You're a terrible liar, little girl." The queen looked at the two men behind Khait. "And what do you want?"

Remembering his place, Paibakamana bowed low and Mastesuria did the same. "She heard us talking about things she should not have heard, my queen."

"And where was this, Kitchen Boy?"

"In the corridor near the kitchen, Majesty." He gestured back the way they had come. Mastesuria nodded.

Teya squinted at him and her jaw muscles tightened. "You spoke of this out in the open?"

Paibakamana glanced at his co-worker. "Mastesuria talked about it. I merely cautioned him not to discuss it out in the open, Majesty."

Mastesuria glared at Paibakamana. "That's not true!"

Teya gestured for Mastesuria to come closer. He took two steps forward, keeping his eyes lowered. She repeated the gesture and when he moved she backhanded him hard across the face, knocking him to one side where he landed on the floor. The rings on the queen's fingers left bloody grooves in his cheek.

The queen turned her smoldering glare back to Khait, pinning her in place. Khait felt like she was confronting a growling lion about to tear her apart. "You, Dressmaker, are a problem.

I believe you make a habit of listening in on conversations that don't concern you."

Panhayboni cleared his throat. "Highness, may I—"

Teya didn't even look at him. She just gestured with one hand and he stopped talking. "No, you may not. We can't just let her go, unless you want all of us to end up on the wood. She must disappear, and quickly."

Pepi stepped to one side where he'd be in the queen's view. "Highness, I can take care of the problem for you."

"If I want your opinion, I'll ask for it."

Pepi bowed and stepped back. "Of course, Highness."

Hori and Merubaste stepped around the others to stand just behind Khait, ready to catch her if she tried to run.

"I apologize for whatever you think I may have done, Majesty," said Khait, glancing at the men behind her before she turned her anxious gaze back to the queen.

Khait saw that the queen was fingering the rings on her right hand, so she had time to brace herself before that same hand slapped her face. She stumbled, but she didn't fall down. Despite her fear, that felt like a small victory. Mastesuria was just now getting up from the floor. Her face now felt wet and she saw red drops falling on her white dress.

The queen's eyes never left Khait's face, and she seemed pleased at the sight of her blood. "Consider my problem, Dressmaker. You are the only person I trust to make my clothes, and the linen you weave is the best royal linen we have. On the other hand, you are a viper who can't be trusted. If I have you executed, I won't be able to trust your father because blood ties can be very strong. If I simply send you away from the golden house, you may find a way to get a message back to someone who can help you, and we can't have that, can we?"

Khait had been trying to hold the queen's stare with her own, but she had to blink, and when she did she felt as if her last defense had fallen. She lowered her eyes, wondering what she could say to save herself.

"So, you have a choice. I can make very bad things happen to you right now, or you can join us. I believe you have some sense of what we are doing, although your limited brain can't grasp the importance or the complexity. On the other hand, I'm not sure what you can do to help us since you are nothing but a dressmaker with ambitions to the royal court. Your father certainly can't help you."

Khait glanced at Panhayboni, but he averted his eyes. That hurt her more than anything. She was on her own.

"This is where you should be pleading for your life, Dressmaker. It could end at any moment and no one would care. You are nothing. You have no power. You are only a fly buzzing around my head; an annoyance. You are not even a threat—who would believe you?"

Khait knew she was right. All she could do was sweat and listen to the pounding in her ears as her heart tried to burst from her chest.

"Do you wish to join us, Fly? I don't want to lose my best dressmaker."

Khait made a small motion with her head.

"Is that a no? Express yourself better—your life depends on it. Do you want to die, or do you want to help us?"

Khait licked her lips, but her mouth was too dry. "I cannot help you, Highness."

Queen Teya gave her a slight smile. "A backbone. I didn't realize you had one of those. I almost respect you for that. Unfortunately, I have no need of a servant with a backbone."

Khait cleared her throat. "I am not a servant, Majesty. I was born to a noble family."

"You're a servant if I say you're a servant!"

Khait closed her eyes just in time. The queen's hand, loaded with her rings, slammed into her face again and she stumbled to one side, dropping to one knee and hoping she would remain conscious. The pain was intense and her blood flowed freely down onto her dress. Hori and Merubaste made no move to help her as she unsteadily got to her feet again, but she felt their body heat on her back when they moved in closer.

Panhayboni took a step forward. "Highness, please—"

Teya chuckled, still watching Khait. "You see? This is how you should grovel. Do you want to reconsider your choice, or are you prepared to meet Osiris?"

Holding her wounded face, Khait shook her head and glared at the queen. Whatever her fate might be, she now felt more confident. "I will not help you."

Queen Teya waved a dismissive hand in the air and began to walk away, speaking with a voice of icy calm. "Remove her. I will decide her fate later."

Eight

1184 BCE—Royal Mines of Timna

Year 4 of His Majesty, King of Upper and Lower Egypt, Chosen by Re, Beloved of Amun, Pharaoh Setnakhte, Fourth Month of Akhet (Season of Inundation), Day 18

\#

Everyone involved in the mine accident was allowed a day of rest. Late in the day, Ray was summoned to the small administration building where Ramessesemperre was housed along with the mine physician and the senior scribe, Horkhebe. Ray was led into the overseer's office by Horkhebe, who looked to be very old and very drunk, and told to wait.

The office of the overseer was furnished with a simple desk and a large chair ornamented with shiny copper on a raised stone platform, two scribe kits that held ink and writing instruments, a variety of notes and records on scraps of stone or rolls of papyrus, and two stools of wood and leather. As he waited, Ray glanced over records of the teams working each mine shaft, the quantities of copper ore removed from each shaft, the volume of copper produced from each smelter, and calculations of projected man-hours required to meet production goals. Oil lamps supplemented the meagre light of sunset coming through the high windows along the ceiling. Clay cisterns along the wall were beaded with moisture, presumably holding water, beer, and possibly wine.

Overseer Ramessesemperre entered the room as Ray studied the previous day's production record for Mine Shaft Thoth, which was where Ray's life had almost ended.

"Ah, I knew you could read. And I saw you taking notes last week," he said in his booming voice. "I assume you can calculate?"

Ray nodded and gave the overseer a slight bow as Ramessesemperre sat behind his desk and swept his graying hair behind his shoulders. Without a wig, his unusually long hair contrasted with the more formal elements of his clothing. His striped kilt was streaked with white dirt. He wore a mixture of copper and gold bracelets on his arms and a beaded collar that hung low on his bare chest. On his left hand, he wore a signet ring made of soapstone with a carved scarab mounted on it. Ray remembered that Hapu had one like it, so he knew the scarab could flip over to reveal an official seal for pressing into hot wax. He studied Ray with his one good eye.

"I'm told you're a quiet one. You do your work and you're efficient about it. The men in your crew look up to you, and you're gaining a reputation because of your bravery in rescuing the others from the mine shaft yesterday. I can also recognize a scribe when I see one, and that makes you more valuable than the criminals that Master Hemesh usually brings me."

Ray nodded again. He wasn't sure where this was going, but

he didn't want to say anything that might offend the man who controlled his destiny.

The overseer stood and filled two cups with beer, offering one to Ray. "Have a drink with me. If you prefer wine, I have that as well, but it's not as good as what they produce along the Nile. Vizier To doesn't want the better wines sent to a bunch of criminals at the mines."

Ray carefully accepted the cup in his bandaged hands and bowed. "Thank you, Overseer, but I am not a criminal."

"And I see you're polite. Someone raised you well." Ramessesemperre sat down behind his desk again. "Not a criminal, you say? Were you a farmer looking for work during flood season when Master Hemesh picked you up?"

Ray couldn't tell him the truth, so he just shrugged.

"Yes, well, that seems unlikely. Not a lot of farmers trained as scribes. And you don't want to tell me more because you don't trust me yet. Perfectly understandable, so I'll tell you something about myself first. Have a seat. I know you must be sore from your injuries."

Ray gingerly sat on one of the stools and drank from his cup. The thick beer had some kind of fruit in it, but not enough to tell what kind.

"Ray, I used to be the overseer for the village of the tomb builders—the Place of Truth. Pharaoh Setnakhte—may he live, prosper, and be healthy—rewarded me with that position because I was one of his trusted royal scribes in the golden house for the first year of his glorious reign. I also fought alongside him in the army. The living god knew that my brother, Baraka, was Foreman of the Gang on the Right in the village, which is why he made me overseer there as a reward. But I was sent here almost three years ago. Would you like to know why?"

Ray nodded, suspicious as to why the overseer was telling him all of this. The way his life had been going for the last few months, he assumed nothing good would come of it, but he still clung to the hope that his luck would change.

The overseer drank some of his beer. "I wasn't sent here because I was a criminal. The Mayor of Thebes—his name is Paweraa—" He paused to spit on the floor. "He made it appear that Baraka was stealing grain and copper tools from the village to cover up the fact that he was doing so himself. The mayor would then sell the grain and copper for his own benefit though Sermont, the Chief of Police." He spit on the ground again. "When I discovered the truth and threatened to tell the vizier, Paweraa offered me a deal without telling my brother. He needed a sacrifice for Vizier To's investigation and he didn't care who it was. If I would consent to take the blame and come here as overseer of the mines, Baraka would keep his position and remain free to raise his family and live his life. So, you see, I am as much a prisoner here as you are."

At the mention of Paweraa and Sermont, the two men most responsible for his father's death, Ray had to force himself to focus on the rest of what the overseer was telling him. His thoughts kept returning to the sight of his father spiked on the wood on the roof of the police station in Thebes, in full view of an uncaring crowd assembled to watch the spectacle of an important man's execution. After a long pause while the overseer refilled both of their beer cups, Ray remembered where he was and nodded his thanks. "I am familiar with the mayor and his dog, Sermont. They murdered my father for similar reasons."

Ramessesemperre did not look surprised as he sat down again. "I see. I suspect there are many of us here from Thebes with similar stories. The old ways are dying and the powerful have become corrupt. Truth no longer seems to matter. When I was a boy, my father was a scribe and he would tell me how the temples were places of learning where I could start my career as a great man, but even the temples have lost their way and all they want now is power. And the gods allow this to continue. Perhaps the only reason Amun-Re hasn't sent Sekhmet to destroy us is because there are still a few people who strive to live good lives. When those people are all gone, our world will end."

Ray sat in silence for a moment. Clearly, the overseer was a wise man who understood how the world worked. "What about the temples here in the valley?"

"Our shrines are different. They represent hope, and the powerful have no interest in this place because it's remote and Pharaoh controls everything. Hathor's shrine is the most popular, although it will need a new priest or priestess to maintain it soon. I've made offerings there myself, along with an engraved stone of thanks to Hathor and to Pharaoh for sending me here."

"You thanked them?"

"I have learned much in this place. There is a beauty in the simplicity and isolation of life here. People die here every week, and it serves as a reminder that we should not take life for granted. Could our situation be better? Of course, but we have to make the best of it. I make sure that our workers are fed as well as possible. When they're not working, they can socialize in the beer house or the brothel. They can trade goods or services to make their lives more comfortable. Or they can just kill themselves after they arrive, which many of them do. Those who remain are survivors, and this is a community of survivors. Which is why I asked you here today."

"Because I'm a survivor."

"I believe you are, and the men who work with you believe so as well. You have earned their respect." The overseer offered Ray more beer, which he gladly accepted. "You met Horkhebe when you came in. He's my senior scribe and steward. He's a very educated man who has worked here for almost forty years, but he will soon be on his way to the Field of Reeds, where Osiris will honor him because of a life well spent. He is usually drunk, but that's how he manages the many pains in his body. I want to give you the chance to learn from him. If you do well, you may take his place when he follows the golden sun-boat into the west."

Ray nearly dropped his cup. "I no longer have to go into the mines?"

The overseer looked amused. "I didn't say that. You're young and you need to learn more about the heavy work of mining, and how to follow the veins of ore, but I will also assign you to the smelter so you can see how the ore is processed. If you understand how these things are done, you may see ways to improve how we operate, and more of the workers will get to know you. However, you will work here with Horkhebe four times a week starting tomorrow. I hope you understand that this can be a big opportunity for you, assuming you don't die in the mines."

Ray thought about it a moment, then stood and bent over in a bow with his arms outstretched. "Thank you for this opportunity, Lord Overseer. I will do as you ask." When he stood up again, he hesitated before asking the question on his mind, but he knew it was necessary. "There is a man here who arrived with me. I've known him for a long time."

"The big one? Yes, I've noticed him."

"I understand that I should not ask, and that you have already done a great service to me today, but my friend damaged his head months ago and needs to be supervised to avoid harm. Is there any possibility that he could serve you at the smelter or in some other job that is safer than mining? His name is Bull."

Ramessesemperre sighed and stood up. He turned to study the production record for Mine Shaft Thoth, and in the long silence Ray began to worry that he had offended the only person who could help them in this hostile place far from the fertile black lands of the Nile.

"You are not in a position to make requests," said the overseer, still studying the hieratic script. "And your friend is a very productive miner. Let's wait another month or so, then perhaps we can move him to the smelter. If nothing else, he looks big enough to haul an ore sled by himself if he can tolerate the sun all day, and that would free up a man for other tasks."

Ray bowed again. "Thank you, my lord. Seven times seven times I fall at your feet in thanks. I will do whatever you ask."

"You will do so in any event," said the overseer, looking down at Ray with a frown. "And you should thank Hathor that I didn't send you back to the mines permanently for making requests of me after I've been so generous. I hope I haven't misjudged you. Be here at dawn tomorrow."

#

Khait was on her way back to Thebes. She had been unable to sleep the previous night, confined to her tiny room in the harem while Queen Teya decided her fate. In her weaker moments, she hoped that Queen Isis would return home from the funeral and rescue her, but that didn't happen. Her only other hope of salvation was her father, and Panhayboni had already demonstrated her lack of importance in his heart through his betrayal—all so he could maintain his position with Queen Teya. She had seen no sign of him since the confrontation in the hallway with the queen, and she didn't know if she would ever see him again. Political creature that he was, Panhayboni would distance himself from Khait as much as possible.

The river breeze blew the long hair of her black wig across her bandaged cheeks. The rope tying her wrists together chafed her skin, and a second rope secured one of her ankles to the mast of the ship, keeping her in place on the deck under a shade canopy. She felt lucky to have any shade at all. Goats, donkeys, and piles of wrapped cargo were stacked around her on the straw-covered deck, but she still had a limited view of the landscape sliding past as they floated down the Nile on the start of their journey to Thebes. There was a small captain's cabin between the canopy and the rudder at the back of the boat, but she would not be allowed to use it. Merubaste was sleeping in it right now, probably gathering his righteous strength for his return to the Temple of Amun-Re in Thebes to be with his master, Bakenkhons.

Merubaste was there to make certain that she safely reached her new home—the Great Prison of Thebes.

A white ibis standing on the back of a submerged hippo drew her attention. About a dozen of the massive creatures stood in a deep section of the river with only their dark eyes and nostrils exposed above the water's surface. Khait knew the stories of hippos killing the unwary who chose to swim or do their laundry near one of the herds. They lurked beneath the surface like the hidden traps of life, unseen until the final moment when the massive jaws opened and the victim was pulled down to a watery tomb.

Khait tried to enjoy the view of the sunlight rippling on the water, the breeze, the buzzing of insects, and the cheerful songs of the birds. The air carried the smells of water, fertile black mud, and green vegetation—a land ready to bring forth new life with the receding flood waters—spiced with dead fish, rotting weeds, and the occasional odor of animal carcass. She wanted to remember everything, storing away all of the details, good or bad, so she would be able to recall what life was like before she was locked away in the darkness to be forgotten.

When their boat passed one of the many small farming villages along the river, where simple mud-brick homes clustered around the temple of a minor local god, Khait spotted a little girl, maybe five years old, playing in the mud and waving at her boat with a big smile. Khait realized then that her face was damp, and the bandage on her cheek was wet from her tears. She knew these tears would come eventually, but they surprised her now, thinking of the innocent little girl she had been, and how that innocence was flowing away from her as they progressed along the river, each passing mile eating away at the life she had known and her dreams of the future. The gods had made their decision, and she was not worth saving. Even Hathor had abandoned her.

Khait got into a rhythm. After a fitful sleep on the hard deck each night, often with one or two goats resting against her, a sailor would wake her at dawn with bread and beer. After breakfast, lost in her thoughts and watching the view go by, she would nap or walk in short circles under the sun canopy where her travel was limited by her ankle rope. Afternoons were much the same. No one spoke to her except for brief exchanges when they brought her meals—bread, beer, and the occasional radish or fig. When they anchored along the river each night, the sailors would start a cooking fire on the riverbank, eat and drink, exercise the animals, and then sleep there or on the boat. Khait was allowed off the boat once each morning to swim naked in the river with a long rope tied around her neck while one or more of the sailors watched to make sure she didn't escape. She rarely saw Merubaste, who mostly spent his time in the captain's cabin unless he was watching her swim, and he never spoke to her. She had no scented oils to anoint herself with, so she began to smell more like the river with each passing day. She also had no face paint, or a body servant like Kemisi to help with her hair or clothes, so she knew she must be looking more and more like a peasant with each passing day. Once every few days, one of the sailors would wash her clothes in the river with natron salts, but she had no others with her and she knew the fine linen would not last long in the prison.

After about a week on the river, two of the sailors looked excited and called for the others as they pointed at a group of larger boats coming toward them. The largest boat glittered with gold and was hung with the blue and white pennants of the golden house. Countless oars moved in unison on both sides of the pharaoh's barge. It looked so beautiful to Khait that it made her eyes hurt. The royal family, hidden behind the curtains in the mid-deck cabin, was going home from the funeral of Prince Amanakhopshaf in Thebes. Khait's cargo boat angled close to the riverbank to make room for the small fleet coming through. For a moment, Khait's heart jumped in her chest, thinking someone might rescue her or that she might suddenly discover an opportunity to escape, but she was still tied to the deck so all she could do was stand and watch this final reminder of her life in the golden house floating past.

Khait couldn't remember the exact day or hour when her thoughts turned darker. It might have been when she woke one morning and saw Merubaste staring at her from the railing several feet away. Silhouetted by the golden sun-disk just starting to rise above the orange horizon, he smiled when she looked at him. The pleated white linen of his robes looked perfect and neat. He wore a beaded collar and several gold armbands. But it was the smile that made her hate him even more—the knowing smile of a predator about to eat his prey.

She knew then that she had a new goal in life. Whatever happened after she reached the prison, she would find a way to survive, and she would find a way to seek revenge on those who had taken her life away. She would not be lost forever, or forgotten, or die doing heavy labor, or lose her mind, or expire of old age in the darkness. No matter how long it took, she would live, and look for a means of escape, and return to the golden house like Sekhmet the Destroyer, Mistress of Dread, Lady of Slaughter, the goddess of war and destruction who raged across the Two Lands to destroy the mortals who conspired against the sun god. As the One Before Whom Evil Trembles, the fire-breathing woman with the head of a lioness, she would burn the air and manifest vengeance so that rivers of blood would cleanse the golden house of those who sought to banish her and murder the pharaohs for their own selfish ends. Queen Teya, Merubaste, General Hori, and her own father had lit a fire within Khait—a fire that would burn until they were consumed by it.

They would know the power of an avenging goddess.

Khait smiled back at the priest.

#

Neferabu, former painter and sculptor of the lifelike images of gods and pharaohs, sentenced to the Timna mines after having his nose and ears cut off for his great crime of tomb robbery, was now blind. After they had arrived in Timna, he had spoken to Ray of his plan to create artworks as offerings to the gods in exchange for other goods and services in the community, but that would no longer be possible. Ray tried to help Neferabu by gathering the traditional ingredients to treat eye problems from the mine physician: fermented honey, yellow ochre, and black kohl. After applying the mixture, Neferabu's condition didn't improve and the evil spirits remained in his eyes. Neferabu was willing to try anything, but Ray and the mine physician both agreed that his vision would now have to heal on its own and Ray would continue to treat him once a day. Ray also tried making offerings of bread at the small shrines to Hathor and to Amun-Re, where Itennu was now maintaining the shrine with the local priest.

After his first day working his new job with Horkhebe under the direction of Ramessesemperre, Ray felt more hopeful than he had in weeks. Horkhebe always smelled of beer or wine, but he was good at his job, even though he took frequent naps. He had started by showing Ray how to find the records and aggregate the production totals from the mine shafts and the smelters so that they could write their regular reports to Vizier To and the golden house. Food and drink were easily available as Ray worked in the mine offices, and he was glad to have the break from tunneling in the earth like a rat.

Back at their group dwelling that evening, Neferabu and Bull were both asleep when Ray returned. Not wishing to disturb them, he climbed the interior ladder to the roof and lay down where he could look at the stars. A short distance from their dwelling, the charcoal fires of the smelting pits smoldered with a warm orange glow, but their bright colors could not compete with the celestial display above him. He had fortified himself with plenty of beer before he left the mine office, so the stars were swirling a bit as he stared into the infinite blackness of the moonless night. The camp was quiet except for the occasional burst of distant laughter from the beer house and the brothel. Considering everything, his life could be worse right now.

Ray's eyes were heavy and he started to doze, thinking back to a time three months earlier when he had been lying in his comfortable bed with a feather pillow in the golden house smelling the fragrant scents of jasmine and acacia blossoms. Pi-Ramesses, the city built by Ramesses the Great, seemed like a lost paradise. He had listened to the crickets and frogs worshipping the power of the great river flowing past on its way to the Great Green Sea. He also remembered the smell and feel of life-giving moisture borne on the night air, and how his friends Bull and Pentawere had tried to teach him to swim that fateful night when Bull had almost drowned. His father had still been alive then, and Ray's status as a royal companion had assured him of being posted to an important job in pharaoh's administration when he was old enough and educated enough to apply his scribe skills.

His thoughts drifted to memories of Tentopet, her soft voice, her laugh, how she glided across the room when she walked, and how any sight of her excited him. She was a lot like her mother, Queen Isis, with her kind attitude and wise comments. He knew a life with Tentopet was unattainable for him because he was a commoner, but he could still dream. He also remembered Khait, daughter of a noble family and dressmaker for the queens, and how she had approached him at the Festival of Drunkenness at the house of Bakenkhons. She had pressed her warm body against his in the crowd, where he had smelled the sweet myrrh in her lovely hair, and the scented oils on her body. Those fragrances, combined with the look in her deep brown eyes, had made him dizzy. He realized that he missed Khait, and there may have been an opportunity there at the festival to get to know her better if they had not been interrupted by her angry father, Panhayboni. He could almost feel the touch of her soft skin against his, and it gave him a warm glow.

He shook his head. All of that was in the past now. Three months had changed everything and the world didn't make sense any more. He had been launched into a journey of fear, exploration, and experiences that were both good and bad. His travels along the river and across the burning desert were like those of a lost spirit, a *ka* unable to enter the Field of Reeds, cast about by sandstorms, unable to control his direction or his fate.

Outside forces ruled his life. And yet, he and Bull were in a safe place where those who chased them would not be able to follow, and that gave him time to think and plan. His work in the mines would make him stronger, and his work for the overseer would make him smarter, or at least teach him more about the world.

Perhaps this adversity, and his acceptance of it, was what it meant to become an adult. Hapu would have quoted one of the ancient wisdom texts to guide him, but his father now only resided in his heart, guiding him from within, and they would not see each other again until Ray made his own final journey into the western horizon. Perhaps his father was among the stars watching him now. Here in Timna, where he could die any time he descended into the earth, he would become the good man that his father wanted him to be, working and leading a life of truth, prepared to go forth with confidence to meet Osiris—Lord of the West and Ruler of the Underworld.

He would also wait, and learn, and if there was a way to escape from this place that no one had ever escaped from, he would find it.

High above in sharp blackness, the blue eye of the evening star winked. Raising his hand, he watched darkness flow through his fingers, a river of shadows, and he heard the dry whispers of time on the wind. In these quiet hours of night, his past supported him, his father supported him, and his friends supported him, and he knew that his spirit could not be destroyed. His spirit would carry him to the gates of destruction—the place where guardians watch over the doors to devour souls and swallow the shades of the dead—and he would turn away with his own strength, avoiding the shadows that no one destroys, and the truth of his victory would make the gods celebrate and give him their protection, making him as brilliant as the sun god shining on the horizon.

In this place of darkness, where men toil beneath the earth, he would become light.

#

I am a man who swore falsely by Ptah, Lord of Truth,
and he made me see darkness by day.
I will declare his might to the disbeliever and the believer,
to the small and the great:
Beware of Ptah, Lord of Truth! –
He caused me to be as the dogs of the street,
I being in his hand:
he made men and gods to mark me.
I being as a man who had sinned against his Lord,
Righteous was Ptah, Lord of Truth, towards me
When he taught a lesson to me!
Be merciful to me, look upon me with mercy!
--Tomb painter Neferabu, blinded by the gods,
Valley of the Kings (Stela BM EA589)

#

THE END

Please watch for *The Revenge of Sekhmet*
(Book 3 of The Harem Conspiracy series) by Bruce Balfour.

For more information, and **to sign up for the newsletter,**
please visit **https://brucebalfour.com**

About the Author

Bruce Balfour, PhD, is the national bestselling author of *The Forge of Mars* (Ace Books) and its sequel, *The Digital Dead*. You can find the full list of his novels, computer games, and comic books on his website as noted below. He would greatly appreciate it you would buy everything with his name on it. As certain characters in this novel would say, "Thank you. A thousand times thank you."

Bruce lives north of Phoenix, Arizona with his wife and a fierce Chihuahua named Bug.

For more information, and **to sign up for the newsletter,** please visit **https://brucebalfour.com**